A TAIL OF MURDER

CAT AND MOUSE WHODUNITS 1

EMILY JAMES

STRONGHOLD BOOKS

Copyright © 2022 by Emily James

All rights reserved.

No part of this publication may be reproduced, distributed, or transmitted in any form or by any means, including photocopying, recording, or other electronic or mechanical methods, without the prior written permission of the author. It's okay to quote a small section for a review or in a school paper. To put this in plain language, this means you can't copy my work and profit from it as if it were your own. When you copy someone's work, it's stealing. No one likes a thief, so don't do it. Pirates are not nearly as cool in real life as they are in fiction.

For permission requests, write to the author at the address below.

Emily James

authoremilyjames@gmail.com

www.authoremilyjames.com

This is a work of fiction. I made it up. You are not in my book. I probably don't even know you. If you're confused about the difference between real life and fiction, you might want to call a counselor rather than a lawyer because names, characters, places, and incidents in this book are a product of my twisted imagination. Real locales and public names are sometimes used for atmospheric purposes. Any resemblance to actual people, living or dead, or to businesses, companies, events, and institutions is completely coincidental.

Editor: Christopher Saylor at
www.saylorediting.wordpress.com/services/

Cover Design: Mariah Sinclair https://www.mariahsinclair.com

Published March 2022 by Stronghold Books

Ebook ISBN: 978-1-988480-57-2; Print Book ISBN: 978-1-988480-58-9

ALSO BY EMILY JAMES

Maple Syrup Mysteries

Sapped: A Maple Syrup Mysteries Prequel

A Sticky Inheritance

Bushwhacked

Almost Sleighed

Murder on Tap

Deadly Arms

Capital Obsession

Tapped Out

Bucket List

End of the Line

Slay Bells Ringing

(also contains a Cupcake Truck Mystery novella)

Rooted in Murder

Guilty or Knot

Stumped

Cupcake Truck Mysteries

Sugar and Vice

Dead Velvet Cake

Gum Drop Dead

A Sampling of Murder

Poison-Spiced Cupcakes

Cat and Mouse Whodunit

A Tail of Murder

Of Mice and Murder

Barking Up the Wrong Tree (coming July 2023)

1

Judith couldn't even look at me. She'd scrunched her eyes shut and turned her face away.

If only I could do the same, but then we'd both be going into her injection blind. Not a problem for her. She didn't want to see the needle anyway. Big problem for me since I was the one administering it.

Judith peeled one eye open. "Pretend I'm one of your patients. That should make it easier."

It shouldn't be hard to begin with. Giving injections was routine for me. I might actually have been able to do it with my eyes closed. But, for whatever reason, administering blood thinners into my sister's belly felt vastly different from vaccinating a Pomeranian. Probably didn't help that, when I gave her last night's shot, she'd yelped like I'd ripped her toenail off.

"You don't have enough fur."

"You're making it worse by hesitating." Judith squeezed her eyes shut so tightly that wrinkles spread from the corners. "It's giving me time to imagine how much it'll hurt."

Right. I could do this. I was the big sister here, and a big sister had certain responsibilities: scare off bullies, bring ice cream after a breakup, distract from worries with teasing. Fix what was wrong. "Maybe I'm savoring the moment. Getting to jab you with a sharp object is payback for all the times you hid my toys when we were kids."

"You never had proof that I took them. You probably lost—ow!"

I withdrew the needle, recapped it, and put it in the special bag to take back to the pharmacy for disposal. Distraction apparently worked with people as well as with animals.

A tear snuck out of the corner of Judith's eye.

I gripped her hand. "Only a few days left."

She nodded. Neither of us looked at her casted leg, propped up on a hill of pillows. Finishing the shots simply meant her risk of blood clots from her post-car accident reconstructive surgery was over. The months of physiotherapy to come probably wouldn't feel much better.

But we'd face that together, too, when the time came.

The doorbell rang out with the first few bars of "Joyful, Joyful, We Adore Thee," a holdover from when our parents lived in the house.

"Do you want to get that, or should I?" I forced myself to keep a straight face.

Judith stuck her tongue out at me. "Toss me the remote before you go, please."

The opening theme of *The Great British Bake-Off* followed me out of the room.

Whoever was at the door rang the bell again. Orion's barking joined in half-heartedly from his doggie bed, as if he was annoyed he'd had to wake up to make sure we understood someone was at the door.

I doubled back, put him in the kitchen, and locked a baby gate across the door. The last time I'd stepped outside to speak to a woman from the church who'd brought us a casserole, leaving him unattended, he chewed the paint off one of the coffee table legs. At seventy-five pounds, he could easily counter-surf if I'd accidentally left anything edible too close to the edges in the kitchen, but lost food was easier to replace than the furniture.

The person outside pounded on the door.

With that kind of persistence, even our long-suffering mom might lose a little of her cool and tell them to hold their horses.

I yanked the door open, and the man almost knocked on my face. He stood nearly a foot taller than me.

I craned my neck back and looked up at him. He had close-set eyes and a cleft in his chin. His face looked familiar in that way that said I should know his name.

Had he gone to our dad's church? Or had he been one of the staff while Judith was in the hospital? This was worse than having a word hanging off the tip of my tongue that wouldn't shake loose.

"Zoe! I started to think I'd heard wrong that you were back in town." His voice sounded thin, as if what he really wanted to say was *what took you so long?*

I kept one hand on the edge of the door. The man's excitement at seeing me was borderline aggressive.

"I'm back." Hopefully the fact that I couldn't place him didn't come through in my voice.

He knew me. I must know him. He had broad shoulders and was only ten pounds away from being considered overweight. He looked like a football player.

Football! His name clicked back into my head. Gerald. Gerald Rawlings. He'd been a year older than me in school, and he *had* played on our high school's football team. We hadn't been friends, but at least he hadn't picked on me—probably because his dad was a deacon at the church where my dad pastored. His parents dropped off soup right after Judith got out of the hospital. That was probably how Gerald found out I was home.

"Nice to see you again, Gerald. Are you here to visit Judith? I can see if she's feeling up to it."

He shook his head, and in my mind, I saw his hair long and blond, the way he used to wear it. He and his dad regularly fought over the length, sometimes in the church parking lot.

"You're a vet now, aren't you?" He motioned back toward a silver car parked along the curb. His eyes were wide and panicky. "We need your help."

I leaned around him so I could see the passenger's seat. The window had been rolled down, and a woman inside the car held a Basset Hound on her lap, wrapped in a blanket. Her face had the same pinched, panicked expression as Gerald's.

There weren't many good reasons you wrapped a dog in a blanket in June.

That didn't mean I was the right person to help them, though. For a lot of reasons. Not the least of which was Sebastian Clunes. If he found out I'd treated one of his patients, he'd cause trouble for me simply out of spite.

I pulled my head back into the house. "I'm not set up to treat patients here. You'll need to take him to the local vet."

He'd shifted to the side, so I had a clear view of the woman in the car now. She craned her head out the window as if she were straining to hear what I said.

Gerald shifted his weight again like he was considering pushing past me into the house and clearing the way for the woman with the dog the same as he used to do for the quarterback on the field.

"We went to the clinic first. The vet tech turned us away. Dr. Clunes wasn't there, and she didn't know when to expect him."

My chest tightened. I clenched and unclenched my

hands to try to release the tension, but it didn't work. Sebastian had claimed Arbor for himself. The least he could do was keep his doors open on a weekday. "Did you try the emergency number?"

Gerald nodded. "While sitting in the parking lot. Dr. Clunes didn't call us back in the ten minutes the recording said he would. We told the vet tech, and she admitted she hasn't been able to reach him, either. She said we should go to the 24-Hour Emergency Clinic. Except it's ninety minutes away. The next closest regular clinic is nearly that far."

The distance pet owners in Arbor needed to travel was the whole reason why my dream from the time I got accepted into veterinary college was to come back here and open a clinic. My dream and Sebastian's. Together.

But that was before Sebastian Clunes decided promises weren't worth keeping—at least not ones made to me.

The tightness in my chest turned to heat, as if I might spontaneously combust. He'd bullied me out of practicing here, and now his negligence was hurting animals. If he failed to show up at all today, that was multiple appointments canceled and pets who needed care going unseen, not to mention the shelter animals and emergencies like Gerald's dog.

If Sebastian wasn't going to fulfill his responsibilities, then he left me no choice.

I stepped out onto the front porch. "Bring him in. What happened?"

Gerald headed back for the car. I followed.

"We were having trouble with him breaking through the wooden fence around our back yard." Gerald opened the car door and took the dog from the woman's arms. "We switched to a metal fence."

The woman climbed out of the car. I'd expected someone petite like a cheerleader since Gerald had been on the football team in high school, but she was nearly as tall as him.

She placed a hand on the dog's head, where he rested in Gerald's arms, as we all walked back toward the house. "He tried to dig under it and sliced his side open. He's been bleeding a lot."

Her voice wobbled.

Having a sick or injured furry family member was difficult enough to begin with. Having to wait for care, be turned away, or not know if you'd be able to receive it at all was worse.

I led them into the house and past the kitchen door. Orion pushed his burly chest into the gate. The gate groaned but held—a minor miracle since I'd been rushing when I put it up.

Gerald made a wide loop away from the gate and Orion. "Is he dangerous? Is that why he's locked up?"

I glanced at Orion. His mouth hung open, tongue lolling out. He didn't look half as intelligent as he was, but he certainly didn't look aggressive, either. He wasn't even barking. "Not unless you're a pair of shoes. Then I make no promises."

Gerald cracked a smile.

I led them into the dining room and grabbed a spare bedsheet from the hallway closet. I flung it over the table. Gerald set the dog and their blanket down on top of it.

"What's his name?"

"Jasper." The woman's tone was breathy.

Gerald stroked Jasper's head. He whined softly.

I held my wrist out to Jasper, giving him a chance to smell me before I touched him. Even the sweetest animals sometimes nipped when they were hurting or afraid.

I ran a gentle hand along his side. "Good boy, Jasper."

He panted but otherwise stayed still. The gash on his side wasn't as big as I'd expected from their description, but it was a good finger's-length long and deep enough to need stitches. I had some isopropyl alcohol, anesthetic cream, a needle, and some dissolvable stitches in the pet first aid kit I always kept with me. I couldn't suture him up without shaving the area first, though, and I didn't carry an electric razor around with me.

I gave Jasper another gentle pet on the head. "He'll need a few stitches, but he's going to be fine. Let me grab what I'll need. I'll be right back."

I headed for Judith's room. I recognized the contestants on the TV screen carrying their cakes up to the judges. She must be watching re-runs. Spending my time sewing up a dog in our dining room suddenly seemed a lot more fun than watching shows where I already knew the outcome.

I hung my head through the doorway. "Hey, Jude?"

Judith tolerated the nickname so long as I didn't break out into the Beatles' song. Sometimes the temptation was so strong that I hummed it to myself to get it out of my head.

Judith's gaze stayed focused on the screen. "Hmm?"

"Do you have an electric shaver? I have to perform micro-surgery in the dining room."

Her head swiveled slowly to face me. "You're doing what?"

I filled her in as quickly as I could. The glare she directed at her cast at the end told me she wished she could assist. Being away from her job at the animal shelter, specifically being away from the animals, was making her grumpier than the itching under her cast.

"All I have is the razor for my legs." Judith grimaced. "Well, *leg*, currently. You can use it if you want. I'm going to go *au natural* with the good leg until the cast comes off the other one. No one will blame me."

I guess that was one perk of having a broken leg. But a manual razor wasn't the greatest option.

I hadn't officially met the neighbors yet. Now seemed as good a time as any. One of them would have to have an electric razor I could borrow. "There's a guy living next door, right?"

"On the left, yes. The right is Avery, and she's single.

You're not going to..." Judith pressed her hand to her forehead. "Of course you are."

I jogged out of the room before she could try to talk me out of it. Wasn't that supposed to be one of the perks of living in a small town? You could go next door and borrow a cup of sugar if you were short while baking a cake. Or borrow an electric razor if you needed to stitch up a dog on your dining room table. They weren't all *that* different, really. I'd give it back once I was done with it, which was more than could be said if I borrowed sugar.

I turned to the left as Judith instructed and rang the doorbell. This neighbor's grass was cut into a checkerboard pattern, a far cry from our one-step-from-a-field look. I swear the grass grew an inch every night while I slept. How was anyone supposed to keep up with that?

A full minute had passed, and no one had responded to my doorbell ring. I rang again. Another minute and still nothing.

I didn't want to be annoying like Gerald and constantly ring the bell this early in the morning, but I did need to know if this guy was home or not. I couldn't leave Jasper waiting forever if I had to source a shaver from a different neighbor.

I raised my hand to ring again. My finger was a hair's breadth away from pressing down when the door opened.

The man who answered the door had to be around Judith's and my age, maybe a couple of years older, with a square jaw and dark hair cut military-short. He had the lean build of a runner. And he had stubble on only one side of his face.

Bingo. There weren't any hints of shaving cream, which meant he definitely owned an electric shaver.

His gaze ran over me…and not in a checking-me-out kind of way. More like a where-was-the-car-accident kind of way.

I glanced down at my powder blue lounging shorts and baggy white t-shirt, chosen because I'd planned to hang around the house with Judith and Orion all day. The t-shirt had dog hair all over it and something that looked suspiciously like a smear of Jasper's blood from assessing his injury. I had showered this morning, so at least I didn't smell.

Still, heat flamed over my cheeks like a sunburn. I probably looked like a crazy person. In my defense, I'd always been much better with animals than with people. Animals didn't care what you looked like.

"I'm Zoe. My sister Judith lives next door."

I stuck out my hand. Nope, covered in Jasper's blood, too. I yanked it back and tucked it behind me. He was never going to lend me anything at this rate.

"I'm a vet, not a serial killer." Smooth. That sounded like I had blood on me because I was a combat veteran, and why would a combat vet have blood on them outside of a combat situation? "A veterinarian."

He crossed him arms over his muscular chest, but a smile flickered over his lips. "Nice to meet you, Zoe the veterinarian. Should I introduce myself with my job title, too, or would that be too forward?"

Was he teasing me? That was better than slamming the door in my face. But was I supposed to give him a cheeky smile or a withering glare in response? Animals were so much easier. Hand lick equals pet their head. Hackles raised equals give them some space. And they didn't laugh at you when you got something wrong.

Teasing, flirting, mild reprimand, whatever it was, I didn't have time to figure it out right now. "I'm taking care of an injured dog. I need to commandeer your electric shaver." I could almost hear both Judith and my mom gasping in my head over my lack of manners. "Please. I'll obviously return it. You know where I live if I don't."

"Okay..." He dragged the word out as if he weren't entirely convinced.

He turned around and headed back inside, leaving the door open. The open door might mean I was supposed to follow him, but I doubted it. More likely, it was supposed to reassure me that he was, in fact, coming back with the shaver.

He returned with the shaver in hand. "Rental fee is a dollar an hour."

His expression was so straight-faced that he could have been joking or serious. Then I caught the tiny crinkles at the corners of his eyes giving him away.

I scooped the shaver out of his palm before he could change his mind. "Guess I'd better be quick then."

I headed back down the walkway to the sidewalk that connected our houses. Cutting across the lawn would have been quicker, but his lawn was so perfect that I didn't dare.

The seventy-year-old man across the street had started watering his sidewalk instead of his grass. He was openly staring at me. Two women one house down sneaked glances my way, their heads close enough that they had to be whispering. Clearly my actions hadn't gone unnoticed.

I shrugged to myself. Some things never changed. *No one will trust you,* Sebastian had said when we were arguing during our breakup over who'd be the one to come back to Arbor to open a practice. *Everyone in town knows it's only a matter of time until you follow in Tonya's footsteps.* I'd hoped that also being the pastor's daughter might outweigh what my biological mother had been and done, but I hadn't had the start-up capital to challenge Sebastian anyway.

I still didn't.

What I did have was an opportunity to help Gerald, his wife, and Jasper—though it might have said something about me that I'd thought to ask Jasper's name and had forgotten to get his wife's.

By the time I got back to the house, Judith had moved into her wheelchair and had wheeled herself out into the dining room, her broken leg sticking out in front of her like a single elephant tusk. She'd also managed to lay out everything I'd need.

I pulled on a pair of the latex gloves from the box of disposable ones we kept on hand for cleaning toilets or working with raw meat. I shaved Jasper's injury site, numbed the area of his wound, and stitched him up. With Gerald helping to hold him still and his wife keeping them both calm, it went more smoothly than I'd ever imagined treating an animal on our dining room table could go.

I stripped off the gloves, and Judith took them from me. "I'll talk to Dr. Clunes' office about getting you a cone of shame and some antibiotics for him. In the meantime, you need to keep him quiet so he doesn't rip his stitches."

Gerald and his wife exchanged a look that clearly said that would be a full-time job.

"What do we owe you?" he asked.

As much as I would have loved to take payment since I was currently unemployed, it didn't seem right. They'd been through enough. And I wasn't technically practicing. "Nothing for me. You'll have to settle up with Dr. Clunes' office for the cone and antibiotics, though."

Gerald grabbed one of my hands with both of his and bobbed our joined hands up and down. "Thanks, Zoe. I don't want to think about what might have happened if you hadn't been here."

Neither did I. Jasper would have made it to the 24-Hour Emergency Clinic, but what about the next pet?

I saw them out the front door and turned back to the mess in the dining room. The bedsheet I'd put over the table might be a loss. I took it to the bathroom and left it to soak in a tub of cold water.

The electric shaver I'd borrowed from the neighbor wasn't in much better condition. It had blood and dog hair crusted in every cranny. It'd probably take me an hour or more to get it all cleaned out.

But first, I had something more important to deal with.

I grabbed my phone and slid my flip-flops back on.

Judith wheeled her chair after me. "Where are you going?"

A litany of lies popped into my head—grocery store, pharmacy to buy more supplies in case we had another surprise visitor, taking Orion for a walk. "Sebastian's house. I don't have the authority to dispense antibiotics from his clinic, and neither does his vet tech. Since everyone says he's not answering his phone, I'm going to the source."

Judith stopped her wheelchair next to me rather than using it to block the door the way I would have done if I thought she were about to do something potentially stupid. Her concerned crinkle line divided her eyebrows. "Do you think that's a good idea? Zoe the Volcano has been dormant for years. I don't want to see an eruption now."

Zoe the Volcano. It'd been a trick from one of the child psychologists I'd seen after my dad got custody. My counselor said we should come up with a code word or a funny name for the angry version of me. My dad suggested The Hulk, but my stepmom, Camille—who I was still calling by her first name then since I didn't want another mom—said that wasn't a girl's name. Zoe the Volcano had been her idea. Whenever I'd completely lose my temper, the idea was that they'd call me Zoe the Volcano, and it would defuse me. I don't know if it helped me deal with my anger so much as it taught me how to hide it better. Mostly.

I opened the door. "I can handle my anger. What I can't handle is knowing other people might need help, and they can't get it. Someone has to make sure Sebastian fulfills his obligations for once."

2

"Sebastian!" I pounded on his door with my left hand while ringing the doorbell with my right. No need to attempt politeness here the way I had when approaching our neighbor about the shaver. Sebastian didn't deserve it. "Open up. I know you're in there."

Judith wouldn't have called this keeping my anger under control, but Sebastian had to be purposely ignoring me at this point. His car was in the driveway. He wouldn't have walked to work. Presumably even Sebastian wasn't irresponsible enough to just go for a stroll somewhere else rather than showing up for his job.

I pressed the doorbell button and held it down. A ringing buzz like an electrified hornet sounded behind the door. "I'm coming in if you don't answer me."

I stopped my auditory assault and listened. It didn't

even sound like someone was moving around inside. Maybe he really wasn't home. Or maybe he was hiding because he knew it was me.

But if he didn't want me to come in, he shouldn't have moved into his dad's old house. I knew every possible way into this house thanks to dating Sebastian in high school. As the pastor's daughter, I couldn't be seen going into his house when his dad wasn't home. And, truthfully, Sebastian *had* always pushed me to give up my *I'm waiting for marriage* stance. Sneaking into his house to make out was the farthest I'd budged—a sore point between us.

Maybe I should have known then that we wouldn't last.

I gave myself a mental shake. The longer I stood out here, the bigger the chance that someone would come along and stop me from going in. I was going in whether Sebastian was here or not. If he wasn't home, at least I could leave him a strongly worded note. Deserting clients was unacceptable. Why hadn't he hired a second vet by now? Done his due diligence. He had no excuse for leaving his clinic unattended.

Unless something had happened to him. Like he fell down the stairs and broke his leg and couldn't reach a phone. Yet another reason for me to go inside.

Curiosity had nothing to do with it. Nothing at all.

I abandoned the front door and headed around to the back. The gate into the back yard was technically locked, but the fence was short enough that even someone my height could reach the mechanism by standing on their tiptoes. I slid it to the open position and let myself in.

The backyard had the look places got when a previous owner had put a lot of time and effort into them and the current owner was struggling to keep up with it. Weeds peeked out from underneath the flowers in the flower beds, and the grass along the fence was a couple inches longer than the grass in the rest of the yard. Fine details had always escaped Sebastian.

The back door still boasted the rusted-shut doorknob that had made it useless in our high school days. Mr. Clunes had always said he left it that way to keep Sebastian from tracking mud into the kitchen from the backyard.

If Sebastian hadn't replaced the doorknob, he likely hadn't fixed the faulty catch on the basement window, either. The scraggly forsythia bush was still planted in front of it, though it'd doubled in size. Hopefully I could wiggle past.

I dropped down onto my stomach and stretched my arm behind the bush. The window looked smaller than I remembered. Surely I couldn't have put on that much weight since high school that I wouldn't fit. Weren't basement windows required to be big enough to escape through in case of a fire?

I wiggled the window in and out with one hand while gently trying to push the lock open with the other. The ancient lock popped out of its track, and the window slid aside. I turned around and worm-crawled backward, going in feet-first.

The drop felt a little farther than I remembered, too.

I hit the unfinished basement floor, and a jolt of pain shot up my ankles and into my knees. I rubbed at the ache. Definitely didn't have my high school knees anymore, though I'd always made this drop in running shoes then, never in flip-flops. They didn't exactly come with a lot of cushioning or arch support.

They *did* make a lot of noise when I walked.

I slid them off. The concrete was slick and cold, like ice cubes under my feet. I tiptoe-ran up the creaky wooden stairs.

The main floor was nothing like I remembered. All of Mr. Clunes' worn furniture had been replaced by modern pieces that looked chosen more for their aesthetics than their comfort. The couch that enveloped you like a hug, where Sebastian and I had snuggled under a single blanket to watch movies, had been replaced by a teal sofa with cushions I could've bounced a ping pong ball off.

An agave plant in a glass pot full of white pebbles rested in the center of the two-tiered coffee table where Mr. Clunes' battered chess set used to rest on a low wooden table. We'd sit cross-legged on either side of the coffee table and play match after match waiting for Sebastian to get home from baseball practice. And a faint scent of lavender lingered in the air now, as if an essential oil diffuser ran somewhere in the house. Gone were the smells of Pine Sol and lasagna that stuck to everything back in our high school days.

Since when did Sebastian start trying to make his living space look like it belonged on HGTV? It was like all the memories, everything I'd been a part of, had been wiped away. Hauled outside and tossed into a dumpster.

And it was all so un-Sebastian-like. The décor of the house seemed at odds with the state of the backyard, as if two separate people lived here.

I stopped halfway across the living room. Two people might live here. No one had mentioned whether Sebastian was living with someone. Nor had I thought to ask since I hadn't set out with the intention of breaking into his house.

Surely, though, if someone else were in the house now, they would have answered the door. Then again, maybe not. I hadn't exactly tried to sound friendly. Or sane.

I picked my way forward. When Judith and I were in high school, we'd been allowed to stay home alone one weekend when our parents went on a couples' retreat. We thought we'd heard someone break into the house. Judith's first instinct had been to grab the portable phone and hide in the closet to call the police. Mine had been to grab up our dad's baseball bat and storm downstairs, making threats.

I didn't want to encounter someone with a weapon or have the cops called on me.

"Hello? Sebastian? It's Zoe. Is anyone home?"

I'd meant for my voice to sound confident, like he was expecting me. Instead, I sounded shaky. Not the way I wanted to sound if Sebastian was hiding in here somewhere—though it seemed unlikely now. We weren't five years old. Hiding would have been childish, even for Sebastian.

And, clearly, he wasn't lying broken at the bottom of the stairs.

Judith had been right. I shouldn't have come storming over here. He hadn't answered the phone when his vet tech called him. What made me think he'd answer the door for me because I demanded it? Sebastian and I weren't dating anymore. We weren't friends anymore. We weren't even friendly anymore.

What I should do was get out of here before he caught me. If he knew I'd been in his house, he could have me arrested for breaking and entering or trespassing or whatever would apply in this situation. And he might if he still held a grudge over the things I'd said about him and his intellectual abilities and that medieval torture methods should be reinstated for cheaters.

Instead of turning right to head up the stairs and poke around further, I turned left for the front door.

The folding door for the hall closet was open. Sebastian's coats and shoes only took up half of the space. No women's shoes, coats, scarves, or purses hung inside. Either whoever he had been living with had moved out or he'd always lived alone and had hired someone to decorate the house.

I reached for the doorknob, and someone knocked on the door.

My skin went clammy, and I skittered backward a couple steps. If whoever was on the other side detected movement, they'd think I was Sebastian and wonder why I wasn't opening the door. I stilled every part of my body, which immediately made my nose itch with an urge to sneeze. I imagined the guards around Buckingham Palace and those human statues that stood on the streets of New York. If they could stay still for hours, I could hold it together for a few minutes.

I could try to inch backwards and sneak out the basement window the way I'd come in, but whoever was out front might hear me or spot me if they came around the side of the house. My best choice seemed to be to wait until they went away and leave through the front door. Then I'd have to hope that Sebastian would think he'd forgotten to lock it on his way out.

"Sebastian?" a deep male voice called from the other side. "It's Ryan. Are you alright? Your office asked me to check on you."

He knocked again, which seemed like overkill. If Sebastian hadn't heard him talking, he probably wouldn't hear him knocking. A little voice in my head said, *Hypocritical much? You broke in when he didn't answer you.*

Besides, this man had been asked to come, unlike

me. He'd be negligent to go away after the first try. For all he knew, Sebastian slipped in the shower, hit his head, and was bleeding out all over the bathroom floor.

Crap. I glanced at the ceiling. I should have thought of that and checked.

"Sebastian?" The man's voice was louder this time. "I'm coming in, okay?"

Of course Sebastian's employee would call someone who had a key to check on Sebastian. At least unlocking the door would give me time to escape.

I backed up as fast as I could without drawing attention by any sudden movement. The door opened.

The man on the other side hadn't had to unlock it. I'd been in the city long enough that I hadn't even thought to check if Sebastian's door was unlocked. Stupid newcomer mistake. Arbor was still the kind of everyone-knows-everyone town where no one locked their doors because they knew their neighbors weren't those kind of people—or if they were, another neighbor would be sure to spot them and rat them out. Someone had probably even seen me climb through Sebastian's basement window. That news would be all around town before dinner, which hadn't seemed important when I'd thought I'd find Sebastian here.

I was still five feet from any cover.

The man took a step into the entryway, and his gaze landed on me. He twitched like he'd been zapped with something and froze. My gaze hopped from his tensed jaw to the police badge hooked onto the belt of his suit to the hand that hovered over his gun holster as if he wasn't sure whether to draw his weapon.

My heart slammed into the front of my chest. I kept my body still and raised my hands ever so slightly, not over my head as if I was guilty of something but high enough to make sure he could see I wasn't a threat. Why, oh why, hadn't I listened to Judith? If I couldn't think of some way out of this, I was going to jail.

"Detective MacIntosh, Arbor PD. Who are you and what are you doing here?" The friendly, concerned tone his voice carried when he was calling out to Sebastian had vanished. In its place was concrete. If Sebastian had been living with someone, this man knew it wasn't me.

Some time since I left town, Detective Stokley must have retired. He would have recognized me and remembered that I used to date Sebastian. He might not have approved of me letting myself into Sebastian's house, regardless of the reason, but he at least would have known he wouldn't need to shoot me.

"I'm Zoe Stephenson." My voice went up on the end like it was a question rather than a statement. I would have offered him my hand as part of the introduction, but it didn't exactly seem appropriate.

His body remained tense. My name wasn't familiar to him, which meant he'd come to Arbor sometime after my dad took a sabbatical from his position as pastor. Detective MacIntosh looked like he was a couple years older than Judith and me. Not a rookie, but not as experienced an officer as I would have expected to take Stokley's job.

He had a slightly crooked nose that, for some reason, made his otherwise average face look daring and handsome, and his suit stretched tight across his shoulders, as if serious muscles hid underneath. His curly brown hair fell slightly longer than regulation length, though maybe detectives didn't have the same rules as regular police officers.

"And what are you doing here, Ms. Stephenson?" he asked.

Doctor Stephenson, but it also didn't seem like the right time to quibble over titles. "Taking care of my sister, Judith. She had a car accident."

Something shifted in his expression. Judith's name registered with him at least. "I meant what are you doing in Sebastian Clunes' house?"

My cheeks burned like I'd leaned too close over a campfire. I needed to think before I spoke rather than letting the first thing that hit my mind fall right out. This was not my day for making a good impression on any of the people in town who didn't already know me. In the city, it wouldn't have mattered. But here, reputation was everything. "I heard that he hadn't shown up for work, and I came over to see if he was alright."

Detective MacIntosh's hand moved away from his gun, and I brought my arms down tight to my sides. Good thing Judith wasn't someone who said *I told you so* or I would never hear the end of this once she found out.

He didn't step aside to let me pass. "Do you know where Sebastian is, Ms. Stephenson?"

His voice still held enough suspicion that my throat went dry. Did he think I'd broken in here to do something to Sebastian? Not that I hadn't fantasized about all the medications I could use to kill him post-breakup, but I never would have gone through with it. Not even to give him a stomachache. I might not be a human doctor, but I still followed the principle of doing no harm. I didn't even eat meat, for crying out loud.

My chest tightened. Part of me wanted to shout all of that at Detective MacIntosh. Instead, I focused on keeping my tone level. "I thought he'd be here. That's why I came. I didn't look upstairs, but he's not anywhere on the main floor or in the basement."

No need to mention why I'd checked the basement instead of the second floor.

Detective MacIntosh raised his eyebrows slightly. They were heavy, but not in a way that made him look like he had caterpillars on his face. More in the way that matched his thick, dark hair and said he could probably grow a chest-length beard if he tried.

He jutted his chin toward me. "Did you hurt yourself in your search?"

"What?" I glanced down at my shirt. Jasper's blood. Along with the original smear, I'd picked up a few other stains. This shirt was destined for the rag bin. "It's not mine."

His hand rested on the butt of his gun. The move didn't look threatening, exactly. More like a warning that I shouldn't try to run. "And whose blood is it?"

3

"I still can't believe he actually thought I'd done something to Sebastian."

I scooped up Judith's dinner plate and mine and dumped them both into the sink more forcefully than was strictly necessary. They clattered down.

I turned back to the table. Judith was giving me a *there's no need to throw things* look that was eerily reminiscent of the look our mom gave when we did something immature. I'd never been able to mimic it—one of the drawbacks of being our mom's stepdaughter instead of her blood daughter like Judith. Some things were just genetic.

"You were in Sebastian's house, covered in blood." Judith shrugged, her tone matter-of-fact. "What would you think if you found someone that way?"

Probably what Detective MacIntosh thought. Sebastian hadn't been in the house, as I'd suspected. As far as we knew, he still hadn't been found.

"It was humiliating to have to call both you and Gerald to vouch for me." I tucked the remainder of the roasted red pepper quiche back in the fridge so we could have the leftovers tomorrow and then pulled a tub of chocolate chunk ice cream from the freezer. It gave me an excuse to keep my back to Judith for a minute. "Where do you think Sebastian went?"

I could almost sense Judith's shrug even though I couldn't see it. "It doesn't seem like him to take off without telling anyone."

I harrumphed. "Maybe not precisely. But when he was cheating on me, he was hard to find sometimes. He wouldn't answer my phone calls. If I had to guess what happened this time, I'd say he was living with a woman recently, but he cheated on her, and she left him. Now he's probably off somewhere with his new girlfriend."

"Maybe." Her drawn-out tone said *There are major flaws in your argument, and you sound bitter and jealous, but you know that already, so I don't need to tell you.* She fiddled with the end of her braid. "He and his fiancée seemed happy, though."

My hand froze on the cutlery drawer. He had a fiancée. Sebastian getting married had to happen eventually, and it did explain the décor in his house. I waited for a tight feeling in my chest or a sting behind my eyes. Nothing. Maybe I'd finally reached the point where I wouldn't take him back even if he crawled a mile on his hands and knees.

Orion padded over to Judith and set his head on her knee. She stroked his ears. "Are you thinking about offering to fill in at the clinic until they find Sebastian?"

Maybe not feeling hurt over his engagement meant I could work at his clinic, too, without wanting to hang him upside down from his toes every time I walked in the door.

I stuck a spoon into each ice cream bowl and joined her again. I hadn't considered working while I was here, but it would make sure we didn't have more emergency cases showing up at our door. Plus, I could definitely use the money.

There was only one problem. "I came here to take care of you."

"I know, but you're going to be here for a while." Judith glanced at her casted leg, then quickly away. "If it takes them a long time to find Sebastian, or if they can't find him...I don't like to think about what that will mean for any animals coming into the shelter."

Her voice was so vulnerable, and for a second, I saw her as the six-year-old I'd first met when my dad finally won custody of me and brought me home to his new family, with his new wife and stepdaughter. The one whose quiet nature and sadness over losing her own dad I mistook for snootiness.

She thinks she's better than me because her dad died, I'd

ranted at my dad. *He didn't want to leave her. She thinks my mom didn't love me enough to keep me.*

Did she say that? he'd asked.

And I'd been forced to admit she hadn't. That didn't stop me from believing it and from finding every excuse to be mean to her those first six months.

I sucked on my spoon long after my mouthful of ice cream was gone. My relationship with Judith changed when I found a stray cat and hid it in the garden shed. "Do you remember Tanglefoot? I think half the reason mom and dad let us keep him was because they were relieved we'd bonded over something. They should have known we were up to mischief when we suddenly started wanting to play together by ourselves outside."

"I'm surprised we managed to sneak food to him for a whole week before they caught us." Judith grinned. "I still don't know why we had to hide him in the first place. I told you they'd let us keep him if we asked."

Lord willing, she'd never understand why. *If you care about something*, I'd tried to explain to her at the time, *you have to hide it to keep it safe. That's how it works. Otherwise, someone will take it from you.*

Like the tricycle my grandfather gave me for my birthday, stolen and sold by Tonya. Or the food I'd hide under my bed to make sure there'd be some for tomorrow and Tonya's "friends" wouldn't eat it all when they came over.

Tanglefoot showed me life could be different, and he became the first of many homeless creatures Judith and

I convinced our parents to let us keep over the years. He was probably why I became a vet and Judith went on to manage the local shelter.

I shoved another spoonful of ice cream into my mouth. "I'm still surprised you didn't tattle on me."

"You asked me not to."

She said the words as if it were the simplest thing in the world to give a person what they needed. To sacrifice for someone else. To trust that if you did, they wouldn't take and take and take until you had nothing left.

I held back a sigh. Sometimes people made you want to be a better person just by being around them. Judith did that for me. Why did finding the best version of yourself have to be so hard? Require someone else to show you the kind of person you could be before you could find enough courage to chase after it?

I didn't want to be the kind of person who sat at home feeling sorry for myself because my love life and career weren't going the way I'd imagined. I wanted to keep trying to be that better version of me.

And Judith would never begrudge me the time spent helping animals or other people, especially not if it would make me happy. "Are you sure you'd be okay with me working?"

She gave me her signature angelic smile. "I'll give you the number for Sebastian's vet tech. She can help you set it up."

***

The vet tech, Kathryn Hardy, texted me to come in

first thing the next morning. She'd introduce me to the office manager, who would be the one in charge of hiring me or not.

I hadn't packed any of my scrubs, but wearing them to what amounted to an interview probably would have been presumptuous anyway. Instead, I picked a pair of khaki pants and a short-sleeved navy blue blouse made of a sturdy cotton that wouldn't show stains in case she wanted me to start immediately.

I got to the clinic thirty minutes before they were set to open. Two cars were already in the parking lot.

I pulled on the door, and it opened.

"We can't keep closing." A woman's voice came from the left, but no one was in the reception area. A door hung halfway open, probably leading to the office. The voice seemed to be coming from inside. "Even if Sebastian didn't arrange for her to fill in, we need a vet."

Her words came out so fast they practically tripped over each other, as if she was afraid she'd be interrupted if she spoke any slower. She sounded young.

She'd also made a big assumption if she thought Sebastian had planned to have me fill in. What I'd said in my text was that I knew Sebastian and was able to fill in for him. Granted, I probably wouldn't have corrected her if I had realized her mistake. Not if her assumption meant I'd get the job.

"I'll still need to check her references," a second woman said, her tone no-nonsense. "She might be someone masquerading as a vet for her own purposes."

I'd heard of people pretending to be doctors before, so it wasn't entirely unrealistic that someone might also pretend to be a veterinarian. I could easily give her my credentials to prove I was certified. The bigger problem was the references. I wouldn't get a good reference from my last job.

If I wanted this job, I needed to step in and control the conversation.

I knocked and pushed the door the rest of the way open. "Sorry to interrupt, but it sounded like you hadn't heard me come in. My first reference is Judith Dawson, unless you think it's too big a conflict of interest to have my stepsister as a reference. She does run the animal shelter, though, and I know you've worked with her before."

The word *stepsister* almost choked me. Judith was my sister in every way that mattered, but calling her my stepsister and adding that distance might give me an extra edge of credibility. Most people assumed that stepsisters wouldn't have the same bond as biological sisters.

The younger of the two women rushed toward me with her hands extended. She had on scrubs covered in smiling animals. The scrubs were clean, but they had a rumpled look to them, like she'd left them in the dryer too long before folding them.

She grabbed my hands and squeezed. "I'm sure Judith's word will be good enough." She glanced back over her shoulder. "Right, Maeve?"

Maeve had to be the office manager. That meant Kathryn Hardy was the woman still holding my hands.

Maeve looked like a taller version of Reece Witherspoon. Same pointy chin and hair too blonde to be natural. Her heels clacked on the tile floor.

What type of woman wore heels to work at a vet clinic? Heels, dress pants, and fake eyelashes. She clearly wasn't hands-on with the animals. Most days, I went to work without so much as mascara, because most owners didn't notice and most dogs tried to lick off whatever makeup I put on.

Maeve's compressed lips and downward slanting eyebrows said that she wasn't as excited about having me here as Kathryn was, but that she knew she had no choice if they didn't want to have to turn away clients day after day, hoping Sebastian would turn up.

She shook my hand. Up close, her makeup failed to completely hide the dark circles under her eyes. "On a probationary basis, and only until Dr. Clunes returns." There was a tiny catch in her voice. She cleared her throat. "At that point, if your work has been satisfactory, we might discuss a part-time or on-call arrangement."

Way to make me feel welcome. Still, beggars couldn't be choosers, and I wouldn't be staying even part-time once Sebastian came back. He wouldn't want to work with me any more than I wanted to work with him.

"I'll give you the tour." Kathryn glanced at my outfit. "Are you okay to work in that? I might have a spare set of scrubs in the back, but I'm not sure they'll fit you."

I swallowed a laugh. No way would Kathryn's scrubs fit me. I wasn't a tall woman, but she couldn't have been more than five feet even. Not only would my ankles be bare, but she was so busty that her top would probably hang low enough to be indecent on me.

"I'm fine until I can get my own."

Who didn't love a job where you got to wear scrubs every day? I sometimes even kept my worn-out pairs and used them as pajamas. But I didn't want her asking why I hadn't brought my scrubs with me. That would lead to explaining about my scrubs being back at my apartment because I hadn't planned to work, and not currently having a job, and a whole load of things I didn't want anyone here knowing about. Everyone, even Judith, thought I was on family-emergency leave from my job in the city.

Time to change the subject. "Do you prefer Kathryn? Or Katie? Kate?"

She grinned at me. "Kat."

Cat? And she worked at a vet clinic? It was too much. I bit my lip to keep from laughing. Thankfully, her back was to me as she pushed open the swinging door between the waiting room and the treatment area.

She glanced back over her shoulder. "With a *K* obviously. Otherwise it'd just be weird."

I snorted and had to turn it into a cough.

Kat showed me the kennels, the x-ray room and surgical suit, the lab equipment, and their break room. I had to give Sebastian some credit, as much as it made me feel like I was chewing on wood and leaving splinters in my lips to do so. He'd decked the clinic out with top-of-the-line equipment, and he'd kept it up-to-date. Even the clinic I'd worked at in the city hadn't been any more sophisticated.

A knot formed at the base of my throat, in the divot where my collarbones met. Sebastian had put a lot of thought and effort into building this business. He wouldn't risk it all by disappearing without a word. Not willingly. But then what had happened to keep him away?

Male voices, muffled by the swinging door, joined Maeve's from up front. Maeve must always stay at the front desk since they didn't have a bell over the door.

Kat frowned. "Our first appointment isn't scheduled for another half-hour. I hope it's not an emergency. What a way to start your first day if it is."

Her speech was so rapid-fire that I had to concentrate to keep from misunderstanding her. It was like she had caffeine in her veins rather than blood.

Maeve yelped "No!" like she'd been bitten—or hit.

I bolted for the front, Kat hot on my heels.

4

I burst through the door so fast that it hit the wall and swung back, thumping into Kat as she came through behind me. She let out an *oof* and stumbled through the door, rubbing her wrists.

Maeve stood with her back against the reception desk, one hand gripping the edge and the other pressed into a fist over her mouth. Tears carried her mascara down her cheeks in streaks.

There wasn't a dog running loose or a spitting cat. Instead, two men stood in front of Maeve.

Detective MacIntosh and Sebastian's father. Neither was even close enough to have physically assaulted her—not that I had reason to think either of them ever would. What was going on?

Mr. Clunes pivoted in our direction. His nose was red like he had a cold. "Zoe? What are you doing here?"

Maeve and Kat both shifted and stared at me.

Maeve lowered her hand, but she didn't release the fist. Instead, she pressed it into her stomach, as if the action could help her hold herself together. "You know her?"

Mr. Clunes' eyebrows pulled together. "Course I do. She and Sebastian"—he choked a bit on the name—"dated. Were even engaged for a while during college."

That was a nicer way of saying it than simply calling me Sebastian's ex-fiancée.

My gaze bounced from Mr. Clunes to Maeve to Detective MacIntosh. Sebastian's dad and a police officer. Maeve in tears.

My throat dried out, as if I hadn't had anything to drink in days. This was bad, wasn't it? Really, *really* bad. Bad enough that my little-kid self would have plugged her ears so she didn't have to deal with whatever else was coming.

Maeve's gaze was so sharp it could have pinned me to the wall. "You said Sebastian asked you to fill in for him."

Busted. I swallowed, but the words still struggled to come out. "That's not exactly what I said. Kat misunderstood, and it didn't come up, so I didn't correct it."

This was a perfect example of why my parents had always counseled full honesty. *There are no such things as white lies,* our mom always said. *Lies have consequences, even if those consequences are only the hardening of your conscience.*

Kat shifted her weight back and forth beside me.

Her face had gone pale, and her hands kept pleating and un-pleating the edge of her shirt. But she didn't ask the question I was avoiding asking, either. Why couldn't she just ask so I didn't have to?

I had to ask. I had to. I had to hear it rather than guessing, even if everything in me said my guess was correct. "Sebastian..." My stomach seized, and bile burned the back of my throat. I swallowed hard. I couldn't say the fear right out. Couldn't put into words the fear that was rattling around in my head. "Has something happened to him?"

Detective MacIntosh's gaze flattened—that look someone got when they had to do the same awful task over and over again until everything inside them went numb. The same look I saw on the faces of some seasoned vet techs assisting at a euthanasia. "I'm sorry to have to tell you. Sebastian Clunes was found dead in the woods behind his house this morning."

Kat sucked in a sharp breath beside me.

My hands went numb and tingly, like they'd fallen asleep and were trying unsuccessfully to wake back up. Sebastian. Dead.

"What happened?

The words were what I'd wanted to ask, but the voice that spoke was Maeve's, not mine. She had one hand up to her throat, clutching the base of her neck. She'd been notified of his death—that must have been the sound Kat and I heard that brought us from the back—but she hadn't had time to ask for details before we burst onto the scene.

"Based on the medical examiner's initial assessment, we've classified his death as suspicious." Detective MacIntosh's deep voice had a soothing quality to it, as if he were speaking to a frightened animal.

Kat was now crying beside me, small snuffles and squeaks that made me want to give her a hug, but my arms hung dead at my sides. It was like someone had severed my brain from the rest of my body. Sebastian. Dead. I'd never known anyone who died before. Acquaintances, yes. But never someone I'd once been close to.

Maeve spun in Detective MacIntosh's direction. She pointed a finger at me. "Ask her where she was at the time of..." She made a strangled sound. "At the time he died. She lied about her relationship to him. She shows up here the day after he goes missing to conveniently step into his place, and she's changing her story about whether or not she said Sebastian arranged it."

A muscle at the corner of Detective MacIntosh's eye twitched, and his gaze shifted to meet mine. He had to be thinking about finding me in Sebastian's house the day he went missing. I was thinking about it. About how my story about going to Sebastian's house to look for him could have been a lie to cover up my real reasons for being there. He had to be wondering if I'd really been there to destroy evidence or to have a logical reason for my DNA to be at the scene if crime scene techs found it there later.

And I *was* the jilted ex-fiancée. If Detective MacIntosh didn't know that whole story, he soon would.

If I hadn't known I was innocent, I might have wondered if I could be involved in Sebastian's death, too.

"Ms. Stephenson." Detective MacIntosh's voice was still low and calm. "Do you have an alibi for two nights ago, between 6:00 pm and 6:00 am?"

A flurry of questions flew through my mind about how they'd narrowed it down to that. None of them mattered. Two nights ago, Judith's leg had been aching, and she hadn't felt well. Right after supper, she'd taken one of the sleeping pills her doctor gave her. It'd been only me and Orion, watching TV together until I fell asleep on the couch. "I don't."

Detective MacIntosh held out an arm toward the front door. "Then I need you to come to the station with me and answer a few questions. Just so we can sort this all out."

***

The cup of coffee and vending-machine package of cookies Detective MacIntosh gave me when he first put me in the interview room were long gone. I'd played through half a dozen games of sudoku and read even more chapters of a mystery novel on my phone. I would need to pee if they kept me in here much longer.

What kind of person forces you to go somewhere

and then leaves you alone? What could possibly require Detective MacIntosh to abandon me here for three hours? Resolving this should have been simple. *Dr. Stephenson, did you have a motive to kill Sebastian Clunes? No? Okay, then you're free to go.*

I shifted in my seat. Detective MacIntosh had pulled out the chair nearest to the door for me when he showed me into the room. At the time, I'd thought it was simply because it was the closest one. But maybe he'd put me here to make me feel like I could leave at any time and consequently wouldn't try to leave?

Could I leave? Maybe I should have already left. Why hadn't I paid more attention in school to the part in my social studies class on the legal system so I knew my rights?

My phone pinged with a text.

How's your first day going? Judith had written.

Worst day ever, I typed, then deleted it. If I sent such a message, Judith would worry and ask follow-up questions. She'd worked with Sebastian the past few years. I wasn't about to tell her via text that he was dead. Besides, it wasn't like there was anything she could do to help.

She'd have seen my "writing" dots now, though. I couldn't pretend like I hadn't read her text. I had to write something else.

It's the kind of day I'd rather tell you about over a bowl of ice cream. And a large pizza.

The door to the room opened right as I hit the *Send* button.

Detective MacIntosh lowered his muscular body into the seat across from me. He didn't crowd me. Somehow I'd thought he would. The true-crime documentaries often showed police backing suspects into a corner and blocking their access to the door. So was the fact that he wasn't doing that a ruse to earn my trust? If he thought I would ever trust him, he had another thing coming after he left me here so long that I couldn't feel my butt cheeks any more.

I quirked an eyebrow at him. "Did you forget what room you put me in?"

His mouth twitched at the edges. Finding my sarcasm secretly attractive or congratulating himself that he managed to unsettle his suspect with the long wait?

He leaned back, giving the impression of someone who was totally at ease. "I'm sorry for keeping you so long. We're short-staffed at the moment, and I wanted to get this taken care of today, but there were a few things I had to do before I could speak to you."

A few things? What did he do—dust Sebastian's house for my fingerprints? He knew they'd already be there. Go search my house for the murder weapon? He'd have been wasting his time.

A heavy weight settled in my stomach. What if he'd tossed our house? Maybe I should have warned Judith.

But no, she would have texted me if police showed up at our house to rip it apart.

Detective MacIntosh went through the spiel about my rights—remaining silent, having a lawyer. It was almost like he wanted me to do one of those things so I would look even more guilty.

The back of my neck itched the way it did when I could sense that an owner wasn't telling me the whole truth about their pet.

I'd ferreted out the truth then. I could do it now. Detective MacIntosh and his nothing-to-worry-about attitude wasn't fooling me. Whatever he had planned, I had nothing to hide, and refusing to answer questions or asking for a lawyer would only drag this out longer.

"I'd like to get this taken care of today, too. I didn't have anything to do with Sebastian's murder, and I should be working."

My throat tightened on the words *Sebastian's murder*, and I swallowed hard. Get through this ridiculous interview, go home, and then I could cry all I wanted. But not here. Not in front of this man who'd probably only think I was faking it.

He leaned forward a fraction. "It seems like you were at the vet clinic under false pretenses."

Where was he going with this? Why didn't he just cut to the questions? "Not giving people information they didn't ask for isn't a crime."

Ugg. That made me sound like I'd intentionally lied,

which made me seem like a liar. Which I wasn't. At least, no more than anyone else.

I drew in a deep breath. "I already told you and Maeve, Kat misunderstood what I said. I asked if they could use a vet to fill in until Sebastian came back, and she assumed Sebastian had contracted me."

He pulled a pen out of his pocket and rolled it through his fingers. "But you knew Sebastian wasn't coming back, didn't you."

Grammatically, his sentence should have ended in a question mark, but it didn't sound like it. He was making a statement.

My tongue felt heavy and dry. The only way I could have known that Sebastian wasn't coming back was if I'd been the one who killed him. In that light, saying he'd contacted me to fill in for him could have been me trying to hide that he was dead.

I searched for words to defend myself, to give him enough snark and moxie that he'd back off, but nothing came out. He didn't even know about Tonya, and he already thought I was a criminal. A murderer.

"What do you mean by that?" The words came out in a whisper. They were stupid. I knew what he meant. But it was the best I could do.

"Dr. Stephenson." His tone was cajoling. "Evidence doesn't lie, and the evidence points to you. So let me tell you what I think happened. You went to Sebastian's house, you slipped something into his food or a glass of wine, and waited to make sure he didn't call for help in time. As a veterinarian, you know about poisons. When the tox screen comes back, we'll know which one you used. While you were waiting here today, I already spoke to a witness who saw you go into Sebastian's home the evening he died. She positively identified you from your driver's license photo."

My legs jittered under the table. I pressed my hands onto my thighs, but the shaking wouldn't stop. Is that why he left me here half the day? He'd been talking to people about me. Interviewing people who lived in Sebastian's neighborhood. Putting together a case against me that would be stronger than Maeve's accusation alone. This had never been about asking me questions at all, only about making sure I didn't run for it.

He spoke with so much conviction. Could the police lie to people? He had to be lying. Or the supposed witness was lying.

"That's impossible." The words came out sharp. "I wasn't anywhere near Sebastian's house since I came back to Arbor. Not until yesterday. She must have gotten her days mixed up. What's the witness' name?"

"I can't give you that, for the safety of the witness."

How was it possible I was a serious suspect in this? Detective MacIntosh made it sound like I was the only person they were considering, and he was moments away from arresting me.

"I haven't seen Sebastian since—"

"Come on. You know I'm telling the truth about what happened." He raised his shoulders slightly and shook his head. "There's no point in keeping up this charade."

Is this what it'd been like for Tonya when the police brought her in for questioning? The difference was that she'd been guilty, and she had a prior record. But if the police had approached her the same way, I could see why she'd confessed rather than fighting it.

I clamped my hands around the edge of the table. "I don't even—"

"I can't make up a witness. All I want to know now is why you did it."

All I wanted to do now was toss my cup of coffee at his too-calm face and storm out of here. Unfortunately, my cup was empty.

I glanced over my shoulder at the door. I'd been brought down here for questioning, but that wasn't the same as being under arrest. So maybe I could walk out of here, and he wouldn't be able to stop me. Right? Staying wasn't serving any purpose. Once I was back home, I was going to spend some time on the Internet, finding out what the police could legally do and whether I was obligated to submit to their questions.

I'd give reasoning with him one more try first. "If you'd let me finish a sentence." I glared at him. "And if you asked me any actual questions, I'd be happy to clear this up. Because like I've been trying to say every time you interrupted me, I haven't seen Sebastian since I've been back in Arbor, and the first time I was at his house was the day you found me there."

"The witness doesn't have a reason to lie. She has an alibi and no motive." His lips formed a straight line. "Look, I'm sure you had a good reason for killing him. You don't seem like the kind of woman who would kill someone without a good reason."

The sassy part of me wanted to ask him what kind of woman I *did* seem like. But he didn't give me a chance to ask anything. He kept plowing forward with his speech.

"So was it because you found out he'd gotten engaged to Maeve? Rumor is that your breakup wasn't mutual, and it was messy. Maybe you couldn't take one more painful act from Sebastian, especially since he also stole your business location. No one would blame you."

A buzzing noise filled my ears. Sebastian was engaged to Maeve? Maeve had been working at my dream clinic with my former fiancé. This was like some weird version of *The Stepford Wives* where I wasn't replaced by an identical version of myself. I was replaced by a prettier, more sophisticated version of myself.

Detective MacIntosh watched me with a fake sympathetic look, as if he thought I was working through my confession in my head. "Officer Coplin told me about your mom. I'm offering you a chance to get out ahead of this. How do you want people to remember you going forward? Do you want them to remember you as a woman who reacted out of pain toward a man who hurt her? Or do you want to be known as the woman who followed in her mother's footsteps and murdered a man in cold blood?"

My thoughts cleared and hardened like ice, even as fire flamed through my chest. So he did know about Tonya. Or, at least, he knew what he'd been told. He clearly hadn't taken the time to read the actual file on her.

I stood. My chair grated backward across the floor, filling the air with the squeal of metal on flooring. Nothing I said was going to convince him that I was innocent. "Tonya Crawford is the woman who gave birth to me, but she's not my mother. My mother is the woman who raised me." I grabbed my purse and slung it over my shoulder. "And as an officer of the law, you should know better than to deal in rumors."

He leaped to his feet. "I'm just trying to give you a way out of this mess. If you confess, I can help you get an easier penalty."

Sure he would. Who cared that I hadn't murdered anyone and that the real murderer would walk free if I confessed. Nope. I was done playing his game. "What's the penalty for being innocent? Because that's the only thing I'm confessing to. And if being cheated on is what put me on your suspect list, then that list is probably a lot longer than you seem to realize."

I yanked the door open and power-walked back down the hallway and out of the station.

5

The breakfast nook table was cold under my forehead, but it did nothing to stop the pounding in my temples. My eyes ached from crying. What had I been thinking to storm out of a police station? I probably looked as guilty as they came. "I let the volcano erupt again."

Judith rubbed my back in slow circles. "I'm sure it's not as bad as you think."

"You never think anything is as bad as it seems." I turned my face, letting my cheek rest on the table instead. "Should I start researching lawyers?"

Judith rolled her wheelchair back slightly and propped her elbows on the arm rests, folding her hands in her lap. "I don't know. I know Ryan—Detective MacIntosh. He helped us with enforcing some of the animal-related ordinances, and he goes to our church.

He's a good guy. I really don't think he's going to arrest you when you're innocent."

Good guy? I held back a snort. She hadn't been there. Detective MacIntosh sounded so absolutely confident of my guilt. "Either he lied about having a witness in the hope that he could trick me into confessing or someone is trying to frame me for Sebastian's murder."

Sebastian's murder. The words still felt disconnected from their meaning. We hadn't spoken in five years, but I'd always known he was somewhere in the world. I used to daydream about him showing up at my apartment and apologizing—for cheating and for the cruel things he said about me during our breakup. We wouldn't be friends afterward, but maybe the nagging voice in my head, that said I'd never be good enough for someone to want me, would quiet down again.

Before Sebastian cheated on me, I'd started to think Tonya was wrong about me. *I wouldn't have forgotten to pick up groceries if you hadn't made me so angry, Zoe,* she'd said every time the fridge was empty. *I wouldn't have to go away by myself if you would just shut up once in a while. I wouldn't have to take the drugs to relax if you weren't such a difficult child.* Everything that went wrong had been me. Forgiveness was impossible. I wasn't worth loving. Nothing I did could ever change that.

My counselor post-Sebastian said all those thoughts and feelings were normal—that anyone would feel that way given my experiences with Tonya and then Sebastian. I hadn't done anything to deserve the way I'd been treated. I was not the problem.

Therapy and a lot of prayer had helped separate out the truth about myself from the lies I'd believed, like silt settling and leaving clear water above it. But the lies still liked to sit there, waiting for something to move through and stir them up again.

Judith scrubbed her hands along her thighs, the scruffing sound jerking me back into the present. "I'll search for criminal defense attorneys just in case, but they can't prove you did something you didn't. Reasonable doubt, right?"

Reasonable doubt was supposed to be how it worked, but occasionally public perception ruled. Jurors gave guilty verdicts for reasons that sometimes had nothing to do with the evidence. Even if Detective MacIntosh didn't have a witness, I did have a motive, albeit an old one. Sebastian had cheated on me. He'd also taken away my dream job. Yes, five years had passed, but the prosecutor could argue that coming back to Arbor woke up all my old feelings of resentment.

Judith would have told me I was being pessimistic again. I preferred to look at it as realistic.

I needed to get out and clear my head. If I kept sitting here and replaying the interrogation in my mind, I was going to drive myself—and Judith—crazy. "I'm taking Orion for a walk."

Judith lifted a hand in response, but she already had

her tablet open in front of her. Search results for Michigan criminal attorneys filled the screen, one with the names *Taylor* and *Fitzhenry-Dawes* at the top. When I came back from my walk, she'd probably look up and ask me if I'd decided not to go after all, completely oblivious to how much time had passed.

I clipped Orion's leash to his collar and stuffed a couple bags in my pocket in case he decided to take care of business while we were out. The house had a generous backyard, but Orion still seemed to prefer to relieve himself while we walked. My apartment back in the city was probably to blame for that.

The neighbor on the opposite side from shaver man —where *had* I put his shaver, anyway?—climbed out of her car and waved us over. Orion and I stopped at the car's back bumper. She wore flowing clothes and one of those new-age healing crystal things hung around her neck like a stalactite. She looked like she was nearing forty-five, based on the tiny crows' feet around her eyes and the strands of silver starting in her hair.

She gave me a smile so big that it looked superimposed on her face. "Hi, Judith's sister."

I scrunched up my forehead. Judith and I weren't genetically related. We didn't look like sisters. "How did you know?"

She laughed and pulled a rolled-up yoga mat from the back of her car. "You came out of her house."

A smile tugged up the edge of my mouth. "You must be Avery?"

Her smile eclipsed every other feature on her face. "How did *you* know?"

I swooped a hand in a way that I hoped encompassed her whole self. "Judith said one of our neighbors is a woman and the other is a man. Seemed like a good guess you weren't the man."

"You can't always be sure nowadays." She winked at me. "Come on over for tea any time. I have some amazing blends I put together myself, and I want to properly welcome you back. I'm so glad you're here, taking care of sweet Judith. I was so worried how she was going to manage after her accident, and she wouldn't even let me work on realigning her energy fields to speed up the healing process."

There was a bit of a pout in her voice at the end, as if Judith's refusal of her offer had offended her. She gave me another wave and headed for her door.

My feet suddenly weighed too much for me to lift them. What would happen to Judith if I got arrested? Mom and Dad had two years left in the missionary field. Aunt Agnes lived too far away and had too many kids to drop everything and come here. And short of Mom and Dad mortgaging their house, we wouldn't even be able to afford my bail. I'd only managed to pay off my student loans six months ago, and I didn't have much in the way of savings. Being unemployed ate through what little I'd had of that. I'd been fired "with cause" so there'd been no drawing unemployment assistance for me.

A man with a poodle-mix who'd been approaching

us from the front veered off and crossed the street. We were blocking the entire sidewalk. If Avery looked out her window, she'd probably think I needed her to alter my energy field or aura or whatever it was she believed in. No way would I know how to decline as politely as Judith had. I'd probably accidentally say something offensive.

Time to get moving again.

Orion tugged on his leash in agreement, as if to say *Less navel gazing, more walking.*

For some reason, when I interpreted Orion's thoughts, they always sounded like my grandma. How was I going to break it to Grandma if I got arrested for murder? She'd always treated me like her real blood granddaughter. What if I went to prison and she started to regret that decision?

My chest seemed too small to allow my lungs to expand enough for me to breathe.

Two months ago, I'd had a job. It wasn't my original dream location, but I'd still been working as a vet, so it hadn't been all bad. Orion and I had an apartment. Our balcony overlooked the parking lot, but it'd been a balcony and not every unit had one. I'd even been able to grow a little cherry tomato plant out there in the summer.

Had I complained about my life too much and now God was taking it all away because of my ingratitude? My dad would say that wasn't the way God worked, but it sure felt like it sometimes.

We reached the main street of town. My brain still seemed full of monkeys all juggling balls I couldn't let drop.

At least the town itself hadn't changed much. The red brick church where my dad used to preach sat at the center, backed up to a park, its bell tower still the highest structure in town. The windows caught the sun, making them sparkle even though they weren't stained glass like those of the Catholic church on the other side of town. Mrs. Grant must still be the gardener because the front of the church and around the sign burst with lilies of all different heights, in scarlets, blushing pinks, sunshine tones, and bleached whites. My dad's name had been replaced by the name of the new pastor—Keith Matthany. Now that Judith was home and more mobile, we could attend next Sunday.

A woman with a little boy in tow stepped out of the ice cream shop in front of us. The little boy had a smear of ice cream on his nose. I hid a smile behind my hand. Some things never changed, and no one would have wanted them to.

I tucked Orion in tighter to my side so that they'd have plenty of room to pass us.

The woman glanced at Orion and me and crossed the street.

My smile died, and a tight sensation built at the back of my throat. She could have pushed a stroller by us, there was so much room. Forget a stroller—a lawnmower could have passed us with room to spare.

This wasn't about how much room was left on the sidewalk. Not this time, and probably not the time before. They didn't want to be anywhere near me.

Had word gotten out that Detective MacIntosh brought me down to the station for questioning? No doubt Maeve had told everyone she met that I was the prime suspect in Sebastian's murder.

Maybe Sebastian had been right when he'd tossed it in my face that no one would trust a convicted felon's daughter.

Orion stopped to sniff around the base of the bistro table out front of the ice cream shop. Normally, I'd let him enjoy the new smells, but eyes seemed to be staring at me from every window now.

"Heel." My voice came out sharper than I'd intended.

Orion came back to my side and turned his did-I-do-something-wrong look at me. Poor boy didn't deserve me being grumpy with him. I rubbed his ear right in the spot that made him grunty-groan.

The worst part of all this was I couldn't even leave town. Judith needed me, and if I left, I'd only look guiltier.

But I couldn't sit on my hands all day, either, hoping that Judith was right about Detective MacIntosh's character. I knew this town and the people in it as well as or better than he did. I'd grown up here. He'd been transferred here sometime after I'd left. My chances of figuring out who actually killed Sebastian had to be better, especially since Detective MacIntosh was already looking in the wrong direction.

How different could investigating a crime really be from what I did now? The animals who came into the clinic couldn't tell me what was wrong. I had to piece it together from what I could observe and the sometimes-slim information I gathered from their owners.

If there was one thing I was good at, it was solving challenging puzzles. And I was tired of people judging me for crimes I didn't even commit.

6

Once we were back into the residential part of town, I slowed down. Before Orion and I reached home, I needed a plan.

Where did you start investigating a crime?

Witnesses, evidence, and motive were what the crime shows always focused on. Detective MacIntosh claimed to have a witness, so I should probably try to figure out who that was and talk to her. If she even existed.

Evidence and motive? Those would be more difficult. As the only vet, Sebastian had spent most of his time at his clinic, so it seemed like the logical place to start investigating his murder. Plus, working there, I'd have a view of the business side of the clinic that the police wouldn't. I might be able to find things they'd overlooked because they were hunting for the quick solution.

I shuddered. That meant facing Maeve and begging her to still hire me. Maybe I had a shot at that. Arbor still needed a veterinarian, after all. But I didn't love my chances.

One problem at a time. I couldn't try to get my job back until Monday, but I could hunt for the supposed witness. Tomorrow was Saturday, and that was the ideal time to catch people at home.

***

I decided to walk to Sebastian's subdivision the next morning, but I left Orion at home with Judith. Not everyone was a dog person, though perhaps that would have been an argument in favor of bringing him: Never trust a person who doesn't like animals.

I stopped at the end of Sebastian's block. Detective MacIntosh hadn't given me many clues about who the supposed witness might be. She was a neighbor. She was a woman. She didn't have a motive. Not exactly enough to pick someone out of a lineup.

Process of elimination, then. Sebastian's house butted up against the woods, so the most likely people to have seen something were the neighbors on each side or the one directly across the street. Anyone else didn't have much of a view.

I headed for the house across the street first. A *For Sale* sign perched in the lawn out front, with a big red SOLD sticker slapped across it. I rang the doorbell. Three times. No one came.

I peered in through a crack in the curtains drawn

across one of the front windows. The rooms inside were empty of furniture. Crap. If the person who lived here was the witness, they were gone.

Nothing I could do about that, though. Might as well press on.

I beelined for the house on the left. When Sebastian and I were in high school, it'd belonged to a couple. She'd passed away from cancer during our senior year. He could easily have remarried by now.

But how was I supposed to figure out if a woman even lived there?

The flag was still up on the mailbox. Maybe some quick reconnaissance would give me the information I needed.

I glanced around, but no one seemed to be nearby. I eased the mail out. None of the pieces were address to a woman.

"What do you think you're doing?" a man's voice asked.

I spun around, letters still in my hands. A man in his early fifties stood at the end of the driveway, a Golden Retriever by his side.

Was it a crime to look through someone else's mail, or only to steal someone else's mail? Why hadn't I thought to check before I went sticking my hands where they didn't belong?

I shoved the mail back in the box. I needed a good excuse. "Uhh, I was looking for an old college friend of mine. I thought this was her place, but it doesn't look the way she described, so I thought I'd see if the name on the mail matched." I shrugged. That looked casual, didn't it? "No luck."

A stab of guilt hit me in the chest. *No lie is worth getting out of the trouble you'd otherwise be in*, Mom always said. *Whatever you've done, lying about it only makes you someone people can't trust on top of it.*

Heat scorched my cheeks. But there was only one way to make this right. "Actually, that's a lie. I was just trying to find out if a woman lived here."

The urge to tack another lie onto the end of that to make myself sound less stupid hung heavy on my tongue. Like I sold makeup and was hoping to show her my products, or that I offered babysitting services.

"No woman lives here." He scowled at me. "I think you should go."

He moved in my direction, and I stepped back. He took his mail, lowered the flag, and headed for the house. He glanced back at me as if to see if I was leaving.

Wouldn't that be perfect if he called the police to report some strange woman hanging around his neighborhood.

Who knew that investigating a crime would be so humiliating?

I headed toward the final potential witness' house. Detective MacIntosh might have lied to me. There might be no witness, and I'd have gone on a wild goose chase. Which he would probably see as a further sign of my guilt.

I'd just have to make sure he didn't find out.

Since attempting subterfuge had failed me and made me look like a blithering idiot, I'd try the direct approach this time. The worst that could happen was they'd refuse to talk to me.

The door of the final house had an old-fashioned doorknocker, shaped like a horseshoe, on the front. I used it.

"Coming," a woman's voice called from inside. "Wait there. I'm not a fast as I used to be."

A woman. That checked one criterion off the list at least.

The door creaked open. The woman standing behind it hunched over a walker.

She peered at me from behind oversized glasses with thick rims. "Yes, dear?"

A sinking feeling filled my stomach. She didn't recognize me. Detective MacIntosh said the witness identified me from my driver's license photo. So she couldn't be the witness, either.

Maybe that was good. Maybe that meant there was no witness and Detective MacIntosh made it all up to trick me into confessing to something. I made a mental note to add "Can the police lie to suspects?" to my list of topics to research after I finished my refresher course on my rights.

I rubbed my bottom lip between my teeth. Whether he'd lied or not, I'd come this far. I might as well ask her to be sure. "I'm sure you heard that Sebastian Clunes, your neighbor"—I pointed in the direction of his house—"passed away. I was wondering if you saw anything unusual around his house three nights ago."

She squinted. "Are you with the police, too? You're quite informally dressed for a police officer. The last one who spoke to me wore a suit."

So Detective MacIntosh *had* canvassed the neighborhood looking for witnesses. He hadn't lied about that part at least.

Impersonating a police officer was definitely a crime. No use giving Detective MacIntosh a real reason to arrest me if he found out. "No, ma'am. I'm not a police officer. I knew Sebastian and…"

And what? And the police think I killed him. And I'm conducting my own investigation. All true. All likely to get a door closed in my face or a lecture about how I shouldn't meddle. This woman was from a generation whose trust in the police was almost absolute.

What else was true and also might convince her to talk to me? "And I'm struggling with what happened." I couldn't have kept the crack from my voice if I tried. "The police aren't sharing many details. I'd like to know what happened to him."

"I don't have much I can tell you." The woman maneuvered her walker around and opened the door wider. "But you might as well come in for a cuppa and a plate of cookies. They're only the store-bought kind, but my hands are too stiff to do much baking these days. I'm Mrs. Murphy, so you know."

"Zoe."

I stepped inside, slid off my shoes, and followed her through the entryway and into the kitchen. The window over her sink gave her a clear view of Sebastian's front door. An orange cat lay stretched out in the sunshine on the windowsill. He opened one eye, then closed it again.

"Fill the kettle." The woman lowered herself into a chair next to the table. "The tea and cookies are in the cupboard right above."

I did as instructed. The cookies were the chocolate-covered kind filled with jam and marshmallows that my grandma always had in her cupboard, too. Some of the tension that'd been making my shoulders feel bruised and stiff ebbed away. One bite of those cookies and I'd be ten years old again, having a picnic in the park. What I wouldn't give for life to be that simple again, just for a little while.

"Now," Mrs. Murphy said, "what would you like to know?"

I set a plate full of cookies on the table. Mrs. Murphy was being so kind to me. Hopefully she'd never find out who I really was—that I was the person currently suspected of killing Sebastian. As hard as I'd tried not to lie to her, she'd probably feel duped if she found out. "The police said Sebastian was killed. So I just wanted to know if you saw anyone around his house the night he died."

The kettle whistled. I poured the boiling water over

the tea, brought the cups to the table, and fetched the sugar and milk from where Mrs. Murphy directed.

"That's what the detective who came asked me, too. I'll tell you the same thing I told him. I did see someone that night, but it was already dark. Sebastian was a dear boy, but he never seemed to get around to fixing the flickering light bulb on his front porch, so I couldn't get a clear look at her face."

The world seemed to shift underneath my feet. Her. A woman had gone to Sebastian's house the night he died. She wasn't me, but I had no way to prove that.

I stirred my tea slowly, giving the sugar time to dissolve. Tea needed lots of sugar and milk to be palatable. "Did she have anything memorable about her?"

Mrs. Murphy shook her head. "She might have, but my eyesight's failed me the past few years. She wasn't very tall, I can tell you that. The detective who came here showed me a picture of a woman, but I couldn't see it well enough. The best I could tell him was that it could have been her."

Were *all* men lying scumbags? Detective MacIntosh said the witness had positively identified me. Mrs. Murphy sounded like she wouldn't have recognized the woman again had she passed her on the street.

At least I knew that if Detective MacIntosh tried to charge me with anything, Mrs. Murphy wouldn't be pointing me out as the woman she saw that night.

Mrs. Murphy dipped the spoon into the sugar. Her

hand trembled carrying it to her cup, spilling sugar. She didn't seem to see it.

An ache filled my chest. Did she have someone who checked on her? Before I left, I'd find a way to work it into the conversation. If she didn't have anyone, I could leave her my phone number if she ever needed help.

The way she'd opened the door to me without hesitation blasted into my mind. I could have been Sebastian's killer for all she knew. I could have been here to eliminate the witness. No one would hear her if she called for help.

I lifted the milk in a *would-you-like-me-to-pour?* gesture.

She slid her cup closer to me. "Thank you, dear. It's nice to have company, circumstances aside."

I focused on not spilling any milk. I'd wipe the sugar into my hand later when I was cleaning up. "Mrs. Murphy, would you do me a favor? Would you promise me that you won't let anyone else you don't know into your house and that you won't admit to anyone other than the police that you saw someone that night? It's not safe."

Her eyes widened slightly, and I could almost see her working it through. "Yes, I do suppose that might be for the best."

7

On Monday morning, I sat on the curb outside the vet clinic. I'd showed up early enough that the birds were still singing, and my hair wasn't plastered to my neck with sweat. Anyone who thought that Michigan was cool all year round had obviously never visited in summer. The high humidity could make you feel like your skin was melting off.

A car pulled into the parking lot, and a moment later, Maeve's shadow fell across me. She stopped in front of me and pursed her lips. "You don't really think you're still working here, do you?"

I stood up and brushed off my scrubs. I'd driven around yesterday afternoon until I'd found a clothing store that sold them. Then I bought five pairs in the hope that my plan was going to succeed.

I bit back what I wanted to say to Maeve. That Sebastian had loved me once, too. That this should have been my clinic. That she wasn't better than me just because she wore nicer clothes and had fake eyelashes.

Stick to the script, Zoe. Judith and I had play-acted this last night so that I wouldn't say any of those things.

"I'd like you to consider allowing me to work here for the sake of the animals in this community. I'm sorry I wasn't more up-front about how I knew Sebastian. I was worried that if you found out we'd once dated, you wouldn't hire me. No one wants their fiancé's ex hanging around."

Dated had been a strategic choice rather than throwing it in Maeve's face that Sebastian and I were once engaged, too.

How had Sebastian loved both of us? The only thing we seemed to have in common was that we worked in the veterinary field. It was like, once he broke up with me, he found someone as little like me as possible and proposed to her.

Unless she was the woman he'd cheated on me with.

The possibility sucked all the air from my body. If she was the one...I couldn't...How could I? Working with the woman he'd cheated on me with would be like walking on a broken bone, feeling it fracture a little more with each step, but going on anyway. How long could anyone be expected to keep that up?

But if I turned away now, wouldn't that be letting him defeat me?

I forced my shoulders back so far that my shoulder blades ached. I could work with her even if she'd been the one, and I would. For the animals. For myself. I would not be weak enough that I let Sebastian keep hurting me even now that he was dead.

The skin around Maeve's eyes tightened, as if she were on the verge of glaring at me, as if she could read my thoughts. "It has nothing to do with your past, and everything to do with the present. I don't want to work with the person who murdered my fiancé." Her voice wavered on the word *murdered*, then sealed over like hardening ice. "Surely even you can understand that."

Even you? As if I were too stupid to understand more complex ideas. My throat tightened. Stupid people didn't get veterinary degrees.

Judith had told me not to lose my temper, but Judith wasn't here. No one could expect me to remain civil after something like that. "If I was going to kill Sebastian, I wouldn't have waited this long to do it. Besides, murders are usually committed by the victim's significant other, aren't they?" I copied her cadence and how she asked questions that weren't really intended as questions. "That makes you a better suspect than me."

Maeve's eyes narrowed to slits. "I had no motive."

The thought that she had no motive itched at me. I gave her my best I-don't-believe-you look, head tilted to one side. "Most people can think of a reason to kill someone else if they try hard enough."

Not that people usually followed through, but that didn't mean they had *no* motive. Belittlement could be a motive, and Sebastian had been good at that as our relationship was ending. Who was to say he hadn't done the same to Maeve? Maybe he had and her ego wouldn't tolerate it.

She drew in a deep breath and rubbed her fingers across her forehead. "Maybe my dislike of you does have a little to do with the past."

When she first walked up, she'd looked ready to haul me down to the police station and beat a confession out of me, fists balled at her sides. Now all I could see was how her lips drooped. Her makeup couldn't quite hide the circles under her eyes, and it did nothing to disguise the puffiness to her face.

From close up, she looked less like a movie-star knock-off and more like a normal person. A person who was struggling with everything that'd been dumped in her lap, too.

The heat drained out of my body. Maeve wasn't the one I was angry at. But Sebastian was dead. I couldn't exactly yell at him. "I didn't know you were his fiancée when I asked for the job. I didn't find out until Detective MacIntosh was interrogating me."

Maeve motioned to where I'd been sitting before she arrived. She lowered herself down gingerly and tucked her legs to the side, even though she was wearing a pantsuit and not a skirt. "I don't like to look like a fool. I felt like one when Sebastian's dad said you were his former girlfriend. It felt like you meant to make me look stupid."

I plunked back down on the spot I'd been sitting.

The concrete was soothingly warm, like a heated blanket. Later in the day, if I tried to sit here, it'd practically melt through my clothing. "I didn't. One of the patients who couldn't get treated here came to my door. I wanted to make sure no one else needed to do that."

Maeve nodded.

I rolled my lips together. I shouldn't ask. She seemed like she was on the cusp of actually hiring me. But jitters filled my chest, as if every cell was shaking. I just needed to know. One way or the other. Then I could move on and concentrate on the work. "Were you the one he cheated on me with?"

Maeve twitched, and her hands curled around the edge of the curb. Her chest rose and fell rapidly twice, as if she were steadying herself. "I didn't know that's why it ended."

I stared at her. Of course Sebastian wouldn't tell her. "That lying son of a—"

I cut myself off before I could finish, despite how much I wanted to call him every name I could think of and then make some up for good measure. When I first moved in with my dad, I'd had the vocabulary of a career Marine even though I wasn't even a pre-teen. I'd worked too long and hard to clean up my language to let Sebastian send me back to it from the grave.

I sucked in a breath to try to snuff out my anger so that I didn't direct it at her again. She could be lying to me, but her skin had paled despite her make-up. "I thought you knew or I wouldn't have blurted it out like that. Learning Sebastian wasn't who you thought he was can't be easy. Especially now that you can't do anything about it."

The silence stretched for one breath... two... until I squirmed inside. Did she think I was making fun of her or something? Why wasn't she saying anything?

I clasped my hands in my lap. "That's how I'd feel anyway. What did he tell you about our breakup?"

"That you'd changed your mind and didn't want to live in Arbor." She shifted until she met my gaze without flinching. "That the breakup was your choice. But that wasn't the truth, was it?"

Another one of her questions that she didn't seem to need or want an answer to. It was my turn to sit quietly.

She shook her head. "I can't abide cheaters. Or liars."

I chewed on the edge of my lip. Maybe I should tell her that I was investigating Sebastian's death. If she found out later, I'd be out of a job for sure, and I'd have an enemy.

My stomach clenched. But then what if she was the one who killed him? Just because someone looked sad didn't mean they weren't guilty. Tonya and her antics had taught me that every time she cried and promised me things would be different. Not knowing Maeve's motive yet didn't mean she didn't have one.

Until I was sure she hadn't done it, I certainly wasn't going to tell her I was trying to figure out for myself who'd killed Sebastian, and that I planned to snoop into the business as part of that.

Maeve stared at me hard, as if she were a World War II codebreaker, trying to crack a cipher. "If you thought I might have been the one he cheated with, why ask me for a job? I barely want to work with you now. I certainly wouldn't if I caught you sleeping with my fiancé."

Answering that one seemed like a narrow, icy path with plenty of opportunities to slip up. My mind twisted into a knot. Maybe I could distract her from this line of questioning. "I didn't catch him in the act. I found a black lacy bra and a thong in his couch. I don't know how you don't realize you're missing those when you go to get dressed but..." I shrugged like finding another woman's undergarments hadn't torn my insides out and left them dragging on the floor.

Maeve flinched. "I didn't need to know that. That image is now permanently burned into my brain." She shuddered. "I hope you washed your hands afterward."

I coughed out a laugh. How was she taking this all so well? Was she actually this pragmatic, or was it not as bad for her to hear about it because it hadn't happened to her? Women who dated or married former cheaters probably had to do some kind of mental gymnastics to convince themselves he'd never cheat on *her*.

Maeve folded her hands in her lap. Her expression sobered. "That didn't answer my question, though, did it?"

My options for answering floated through my mind like cue cards. I shuffled through them looking for something that would be truthful enough to convince her without having to reveal everything. One answer might work.

I cupped my hands over my knees. "It was always my dream to work as a vet in Arbor. Sebastian hadn't even considered becoming a vet himself until I told him that was my plan. Not that he didn't love animals. He did. But it always felt like he saw something I had, decided he wanted it, and then took it from me. I want it back."

It was the truth, even if it wasn't the full truth. Based on how Maeve had reacted to my previous omission, she probably wouldn't be convinced by the distinction. I'd just have to make sure she never found out.

Maeve sat so still that I was sure her insides were churning at faster-than-light speeds. "It won't be the same. This won't be your business."

Way to rub glass shards into an open wound. She was going to be a joy to work with.

That snarky reply jumped to my lips, and I bit the inside of my cheek to hold it back. Do not rise to the bait. "That doesn't mean the animals in Arbor need veterinary care any less."

"I vote for keeping her."

Maeve and I both jerked. Kat stood in front of us, clutching her purse to her belly. She wore a different pair of rumpled scrubs, light purple covered in yellow ducks this time.

"This isn't a democracy, Kat." Maeve's voice sounded the way an eyeroll looked. "And she's not a stray cat we're adopting."

Kat shrugged. "No, but if we don't get a vet in, we'll have to close." Her gaze skittered to the side and back to Maeve. "I can't afford to be out of a job."

Maeve's lips drew into a thin line, and her eyes narrowed, as if she wanted both of us to be sure that this wasn't going to be the new norm. She was still the boss. "On probationary status." She turned her gaze to me again, and the force of it could have cut through my bones. "But if the police find any evidence linking you to Sebastian's murder, you're done."

8

"Zoe?"

Uh-oh. My name as a question was never a good sign. Neither was the tentative note in Judith's voice.

I spun our home office chair around. My eyes needed a rest from staring at the screen anyway, from reading about all the things the police could and couldn't do. Lying to a suspect was apparently completely allowable. So Detective MacIntosh hadn't been breaking any laws when he'd lied to me. That didn't make me feel any better about it.

Judith's wheelchair whirred, followed by a thump like rubber hitting wood. "Gah! Why did they make doors so narrow in the 1950s? I'm going to be bored to death of the three rooms I can fit in by the time this is over. You're going to have to come to me."

The hesitant expression on her face said I wasn't

going to like what I found when I got there. I heaved myself out of the chair and went to her side.

Judith cradled something in her hands that looked suspiciously like my cell phone, minus its case.

My shoulders slumped. "Oh no."

Judith bit her bottom lip in an I'm-so-sorry face. "I think the case protected it mostly. The case is in about six pieces on the floor. I couldn't reach them. Orion spit your actual phone out into my hand when I told him to give it."

That was some improvement, at least. When I'd originally adopted him and he'd stolen something, he'd run from me when I tried to get it back, tail between his legs and teeth clamped tightly shut around my socks or a DVD case. Even a can of pop once, sticky liquid leaking in a trail behind him.

I took the phone from Judith. The screen had a smear of Orion drool across it. I wiped it on my pants and pressed the home button. The screen flickered and went dark.

Crap.

I pressed the button again, but it didn't even try to come to life this time. Not good. On so many levels.

"He knew I was upset with him." Judith wheeled away from the doorway, making room for me to come out. "He's on his bed with his head on his paws giving me the *Do you still love me?* look."

I knew that look well. "It's only partially his fault. He's an emotional barometer, and we've been under a lot of stress. I should have known better than to leave my phone on the end table. I should have put it on the bookcase or in a drawer or something."

"It could be worse." Judith shrugged. "He could be one of those dogs who poops in your shoes when he's upset."

"Cats do that more than dogs."

Judith snort-laughed. "I never thought I'd be glad we didn't have a cat."

I glared at my paperweight of a phone. My phone plan was nowhere near giving me an upgraded phone for free. And I definitely didn't have hundreds of dollars to drop on a new one.

"Is there a repair shop in town?"

Judith gave me directions, and I snapped Orion's leash on. He clearly needed more exercise to wear him out. That, and I couldn't trust him home alone with Judith. If he decided to go for the TV remote next, she wouldn't be able to move fast enough to stop him.

The cell phone repair shop ended up being on the main street, not too far from the ice cream shop where we'd been snubbed last time. I'd made a point of walking in the opposite direction since our double snubbing last week. Time to rip off the avoidance band-aid.

I held my head high and passed the ice cream shop. The bistro tables outside were full on a Saturday. I kept my gaze focused straight ahead and hummed to myself a little so I wouldn't accidentally overhear anything in case someone decided to comment on me.

The repair shop was a sliver of a building, about half the size of anything else on the street. The hours on the door said they should be open, but the shop was dark.

I pulled on the door. Locked.

I pressed my face close to the window. If I could spot someone and wave, maybe they'd let me in. Phone cases and screen protectors lined one wall, while a colorful selection of cords and security system boxes were displayed on the other. But the lights were definitely off, and there was no sign of movement inside.

"Hey," a semi-familiar man's voice said. "It's the shaver thief."

I spun around and barely stopped myself before tripping over Orion, who'd apparently dropped to the sidewalk directly behind me. Thank goodness I'd always had excellent balance. Otherwise, I would have wiped out and taken the man with me. I'd done enough embarrassing things since coming home. I didn't need to add tackling a stranger to the list.

I lifted my gaze. The neighbor I'd borrowed the electric razor from stood on the other side of Orion. He'd swapped his pajama pants and t-shirt for running shorts and a tight black t-shirt that made his eyes seem an unnatural shade of blue and showed off his lean arms.

My palms went sweaty. Had he been this good-looking the other morning?

I yanked my gaze away. The last thing I needed was

to be ogling a man who thought I was a thief. Only rejection could come from that. "I didn't steal it. I'm going to return it." Now that I remembered I still had it. Really, between Sebastian's death, being questioned by the police, and trying to get a job, forgetting a few things wasn't unreasonable. Hopefully the crusted-on gunk would come off after it'd been stuffed somewhere for over a week. "I just need to clean it up. I didn't think you'd want it back covered in blood and dog hair."

His lips twisted in what could have either been a wry smile or a grimace. "On second thought, I'll buy a new one or stick with my manual razor. You can keep the one you borrowed." He smiled in a way that crinkled his eyes. "Just in case another emergency shows up at your door."

There wasn't any real accusation or sarcasm in his voice. Maybe I'd jumped to conclusions about him thinking I was a thief. He might have been joking, and I just missed it.

My skin felt too hot for comfort. I shouldn't have jumped to conclusions about him, but apologizing for something he didn't even know I'd done seemed like it would only make things more awkward.

I pointed back over my shoulder at the cell phone repair shop. "Do you know if they're still open for business?"

My neighbor ran a hand over his short hair. "As of last week they were, but Jack repairs all kinds of electronics. He's probably out at someone's house right now."

Perfect. I'd been hoping he'd be able to fix my phone while I waited. "Do you know how I can—"

"That animal needs to be muzzled in public!" The woman's voice shouting from across the street had the tone of someone who expected to be obeyed.

My neighbor turned, and I stepped around Orion. I hadn't intended to put myself between him and whoever was yelling, but I wasn't sad it worked out that way, either. The last thing Orion needed when he was already stressed was to feel threatened, too. We'd gone months since his last nightmare where he cried or growled in his sleep.

A woman in her mid-forties stalked across the street, straight for us, not even checking for traffic, as if she expected the cars would yield to her. She looked like she'd stepped out of a corny adventure novel, with purple rubber boots that came up to her knees, a floppy hat, and a tank top. She also had a sheer purple scarf looped around her neck—not the most sensible fashion choice for the heat of late June. Her walking stick rapped the ground with each step.

A girl of maybe eight or nine waited on the other side of the street, holding the leash of a dog no bigger than Orion's head. The girl's outfit matched the woman's, minus the scarf.

Orion scrambled to his feet and pressed against my leg. His tail gave the low, slow wag that a lot of people misinterpreted as friendliness but actually meant the opposite. The lower and slower a tail swung, the more tense and uncertain a dog was. Anything that looked like a stick could still trigger him into hyper-alertness, and the woman thumped her walking stick on the ground as if she meant to crack the concrete.

She stopped in front of us, and the fur on the back of Orion's neck stood up.

Strands of hair the same dark brown as mine were plastered to her forehead under the brim of her hat, and sweat beaded her upper lip as if she'd just finished a long hike. "Did you hear me?"

I dropped a hand to Orion's back. He glanced up at me, and his muscles relaxed slightly under my touch. *That's right, buddy. Ignore the crazy lady.* "I think you might have us confused with someone else."

The woman motioned toward Orion with her stick. He flinched backward, and his ears flattened against his head. His tail froze.

She kept the stick pointed at us like a sword. "We don't allow pit bulls in this town. If you're just passing through, you're required by law to muzzle your animal any time it's out in public."

Orion backed away until he was most of the way under a table. I let his leash slide through my fingers to give him the space he needed to feel safe.

My blood pumped so loudly in my ears that I almost couldn't hear myself think. Should I defend Orion—who wasn't even in the pit bull family—or demand that this woman explain herself? Really, what kind of person accosts a stranger on the street?

At least I knew now why people had crossed to the other side of the road on our previous walks. It hadn't been about me at all. Someone had fanned the people of this town into unwarranted fear over certain breeds of dogs, and they mistook Orion for one of those breeds.

My heart beat painfully fast in my chest. One part of me wanted to educate this woman—and the whole town, for that matter. Statistically speaking, dog bites had nothing to do with whether certain breeds were banned and everything to do with proper owner education and training.

The words jumped to my lips, but I could almost hear Judith whispering in my ear that this wasn't the time or place. If I let my temper get the best of me and shamed this woman publicly, she wouldn't listen to anything I had to say.

I sucked a deep breath in through my nose and let it out through my mouth. "Last I checked, Michigan doesn't have a law banning"—I made air quotes with my fingers—"*dangerous breeds*. And even if it did, my dog is a Boxer. Boxers aren't banned anywhere. In the world."

Judith probably would have told me I was still too sarcastic, but my neighbor raised a hand to his mouth as if he were hiding a smile.

The woman shifted the scarf around her neck. "Towns are allowed to enact their own regulations to keep the public safe. If you want to walk that..." She sniffed. "That *thing* around, without a muzzle, you'll need to provide proof it's not one of the breeds on the list."

That *thing*? As if he were an alien species, and as if I hadn't told her less than thirty seconds ago that Orion was a Boxer. He probably wasn't a purebred Boxer, but that's what anyone with working eyes who looked at him would see.

My neighbor held up his phone and angled the screen toward the woman. He'd pulled up a picture of a Boxer. "I don't think extra proof is necessary. Her dog looks exactly like the picture of a Boxer on the American Kennel Club website, don't you agree?"

A little tug in my chest had me leaning fractionally toward him. He stood up for me and Orion. And not in that patronizing way that some people had of jumping to your defense that left you feeling like they thought you couldn't stick up for yourself. More in an allies-in-the-same-battle kind of way.

The woman drew herself up, as if by standing slightly taller she could intimidate him into backing down. She angled her walking stick so the end pointed in his direction like an overly large finger wagging at him. "Mind your own business, Pastor." She pushed each word out like a jab. "You worry about the church, and I'll worry about the town."

Pastor? The tugging feeling in my chest snapped, and I stepped backward a fraction.

Judith was going to get an earful when I got home

about leaving that detail out. I'd almost considered flirting with him. Or, at least, not shutting him down if he thought about flirting with me, which was where it seemed like his teasing might be heading.

But pastors weren't supposed to casually flirt, and they certainly didn't date women they wouldn't consider marriage material. I'd make a terrible pastor's girlfriend, let alone wife. I wasn't soft-spoken and easygoing like Judith or Mom. I had a biological mother in prison, and my last job... well, it'd be the proverbial straw for the proverbial camel.

Besides, I wouldn't be here long. I could date again when I got back to the city.

My neighbor-pastor's face had gone still, and his eyes looked hard around the edges. The way he stood reminded me more of a police officer than a pastor. "As a member of the town council, it *is* my business, Madam Mayor."

I squeezed my eyes shut. Great. This had to be what people meant when they said you could never go home again. Our attractive next-door neighbor was a pastor and therefore off limits, the police wanted to put me in prison, and the mayor of the town was unhinged and out for blood—Orion's blood.

"I think it's time we stop postponing revisiting the ban." His voice wasn't raised or confrontational. He stated the words matter-of-factly. "And put it back on the agenda for the next meeting."

The mayor harrumphed, pivoted on her heel, and marched back across the road.

Orion slunk close to me again and pressed his dry nose into my hand. He still held his tail low, as if he wasn't sure the threat had passed.

I stroked his head. How could she think Orion was dangerous when he'd practically run away from her? The only way he'd ever bite someone was if they literally backed him into a corner and he felt he had no other way out, or if they were hurting me. But that'd be functionally the same as self-defense.

Madam Mayor grabbed her daughter's hand and the leash to her own dog without slowing down.

I turned back to my neighbor... the pastor. "She seems intense."

He rubbed the back of his neck, but the muscles there stayed so tight that the cords stood out. "One of the first things she did after she was elected was push through a breed-specific ban. She invited people who'd been bitten to tell their stories, and the regulation passed easily."

He didn't say whether he'd been on the council at that time or how he'd voted.

He sighed. "It seemed like a positive thing at first. It's gotten out of hand lately, with her trying to personally enforce everything, and then we had an issue recently when a pit bull was picked up by animal control."

"Judith told me about that, I think. The dog had gotten loose somehow, and he ended up at the shelter?

The owner swore the dog wasn't a pit bull, right up until a DNA test proved he was. He had to be adopted out of town."

Neighbor-pastor-guy nodded and shifted his gaze to watch the mayor turn the corner. "There were some threats of violence against the shelter, and pressure from outside the town to overturn the ban. We were supposed to revisit it at the next town council meeting, but then Judith had her car accident. It was shelved for the time being since the council wanted to hear from her as the shelter's manager."

My heart kicked against the front of my chest. Judith hadn't told me that there'd been threats against the shelter. It was one thing to be the family optimist. It was another thing entirely to downplay potential violence.

"I don't think Jack's coming back today." He hooked his thumb toward the cell phone repair shop. "Do you want me to take a quick look?"

I quirked an eyebrow at him. "You're a pastor, on the town council, and you fix electronics?"

He shrugged, and that grin of his was back—the one that made it suddenly hard for me to breathe. "I was in the military. I'm used to keeping busy." He winked at me. "My name's Keith."

Keith, as in Pastor Keith Matthany, who'd taken my dad's place after he went on sabbatical from the pastorate to go into missionary work. I would have already known who he was if I hadn't skipped church with the excuse of needing to take care of Judith for the two Sundays since I'd been back.

Heat spread across my cheeks, and I dropped my gaze to my purse. It was like he knew the pastor part was making me uncomfortable. It shouldn't have. I was a Christian, after all. And my dad was a pastor.

I just wasn't used to finding a pastor so attractive, and Keith—Pastor Keith—seemed to know it.

I thrust my phone out more forcefully than I probably needed to and plastered a stern expression on my face. Frankly, he shouldn't keep teasing or flirting or whatever it was. That wasn't very pastor-like of him.

He examined my phone. "Do you have a pair of tweezers?"

What was this, phone surgery? "Somewhere. I carry a pair in case Orion gets something stuck in his paw pads."

I yanked open my purse and fished around. Barrow's solution for Orion's ears, to keep them from getting inflamed. I handed it over.

Benadryl in case Orion got stung by a hornet. Gauze pads in sterile packaging. Cat toenail clippers. A tick remover. I wasn't going to find anything with my purse this full. I passed them all over to Pastor Keith, too, and shoved my hand down to the bottom.

My fingers brushed against something thin and hard. "Found 'em."

I looked up.

He was staring down at the collection of items in his

hands. "You regularly carry all this around with you?"

His voice had a glazed tone to it, like I might even be above and beyond in preparedness than someone in the military.

I shrugged. "I don't like to be caught off-guard."

He dumped all my belongings back into my purse and accepted the tweezers. "I can see that."

He did something with the tweezers and my phone that I couldn't follow. The screen came back on.

He handed it back to me. "It won't be permanent, but at least now you'll be able to call Jack and set up an appointment." He pointed to the phone number painted on the window. "See you around the neighborhood, Zoe the veterinarian."

I flinched. Knowing that he was an actual military veteran, I'd probably sounded even more of an idiot that first day we met when I felt the need to explain that, when I said I was a vet, I meant veterinarian, not military veteran.

My phone showed two missed calls. The most recent one was from Judith—probably calling to see if I'd gotten my phone fixed since I'd been gone for a while now. The second was from a number with a foreign area code. That had to be our parents. Figures I'd miss their call. Yet another reason I needed to get this thing fixed sooner rather than later.

My phone rang before I could send Judith a quick text or call Jack. The name of a law firm scrolled across caller ID.

My throat burned, and I touched the window of the cell phone repair shop to steady myself. Judith had said she was going to research lawyers just in case. She must have made some calls and found out that I was in a lot of trouble.

I slid my finger across the screen to answer. "Hello?" My voice came out as a squeak.

"This is Danica Dickerson with the law firm of Page and Sketchley." Ms. Dickerson's voice was raspy, like a smoker's. "Is this Zoe Stephenson?" She rattled off the address of my apartment in the city.

My heart raced so fast that my head felt light. "That's me."

"We were retained by your maternal grandfather, William Crawford, to execute his estate. I'd like to set up an appointment for a video call with you and your sister since you're out of state."

I slumped my whole body against the side of the building. This wasn't about me being accused of Sebastian's murder. A possible inheritance was a good thing.

I'd only met my maternal grandfather a couple of times. He'd basically disowned Tonya, so it wasn't until I moved in with my dad that I even met him. And he lived across the country, meaning our visits were few and far between. When his nursing home called me a few weeks ago to tell me he'd passed away, I hadn't even considered he might have left me something. Or that he would have had anything left to leave after pre-paying his own funeral and his years in a care facility.

The inheritance must be small. And Ms. Dickerson had said she needed to speak to me and Judith. Which was a bit odd. Judith wasn't his biological granddaughter. Not that blood made family, but my grandfather had seemed like the kind of man that might matter to.

I rifled through my purse and came up with a pen and a receipt to write on. "I can set up something for my sister and me."

"Excellent. How about—"

Silence filled my ear. I looked at the phone screen. Black. Pastor Keith hadn't been kidding when he said my phone wouldn't last long.

Hopefully Danica Dickerson wouldn't think I'd hung up on her. I couldn't even call her back without access to my phone's call log. The best I could do was try searching for her law firm on the Internet, or wait until I could get Jack to fix my phone.

I clucked at Orion, and he climbed back to his feet.

An inheritance. And just this morning I'd been thinking I'd kill to have enough to fix my phone.

My mouth went dry, and I stopped. People did kill for inheritances. That's what had been bothering me ever since Maeve told me she had no reason to kill Sebastian. Someone had inherited everything Sebastian had, including the house and the veterinary practice. Those weren't small things.

If Maeve inherited all of Sebastian's possessions, she definitely had a motive. And I knew how I could find out.

9

Sebastian's dad lived in an apartment complex called Riverside Gardens, even though there didn't seem to be any gardens and it was nowhere near a river. The complex was two stories, and the sign out front declared it only allowed residents fifty and over. Even from the outside, the building had a calm, mature air with its dark red brick and tidy front walk free of litter or weeds. The *They Poop, You Scoop* sign with a squatting dog on it and free baggies underneath showed how serious they were about cleaning up.

The front door of the building was locked. Next to it, a panel of names and buttons allowed visitors to contact a resident to buzz in their guests.

Mr. Clunes' name was in the first row of buttons. A sharp, tight sensation built in the center of my chest.

What kind of person intruded on someone else's

grief to save their own skin? A selfish one, that's what kind. Someone who ranked right up there with con artists, used car salesmen, and reporters on the sleaze scale.

The names on the panel blurred. What if he believed I'd killed Sebastian? He hadn't said anything when Detective MacIntosh told me I needed to come down to the station for questioning. He'd just stood there, looking dazed, like a person trying to watch a foreign movie without subtitles.

My mind flooded with memories of Mr. Clunes helping my dad move me into an apartment when I went to veterinary college, of the pair of soft mittens he gave me every Christmas because he knew I had a habit of losing mine, of how he always wanted to talk to me, too, if I was at Sebastian's when he called.

No amount of therapy would fix it—fix me—if I looked at him and saw that he believed I killed Sebastian.

Orion touched his nose to my hand as if to say *Let's just go home and forget this nonsense*. He was right, even if he was a dog. There had to be a better way to find out if Maeve inherited Sebastian's house and clinic. And likely she hadn't. Everything had probably gone to Mr. Clunes, and nothing could have induced him to kill for it.

"Who are you looking for?" a man's voice said from behind me. "Maybe I can help."

A voice I knew. Like Sebastian's, only more weathered around the edges.

It was like my fears had conjured him out of thin air.

I turned around so slowly I almost felt like I wasn't moving. Mr. Clunes' face was puffy and unshaven, and his shirt was untucked on one side. Under his arm, he carried a box of something from his favorite place—True Loaf Bakery.

"I didn't kill him." The words spilled out before I could stop them. "I know what the police are saying, but it wasn't me."

My voice sounded phlegmy by the end, and my throat was tight.

"Oh, Zoe-girl." He opened his arms, box and all. "I know. I know you."

I dragged Orion behind me and stumbled into his hug. He smelled faintly of alcohol.

Tears I hadn't even known I'd been holding in poured out. When I finally pulled away, his pale blue shirt had a dark blue water mark near the shoulder.

I really was an awful person. Not only had I planned to come here and pump him for information, but now he'd ended up comforting me when I hadn't even seen Sebastian in five years, whereas he'd lost his only child.

He punched a code into the door and opened it for me. "Come on in. I have a fresh box of donuts. We can eat the whole dozen, and no one will be the wiser."

I half laughed but choked on it. I'd always been Mr. Clunes' partner-in-crime when he wanted an excuse to buy something unhealthy despite his high cholesterol. *Zoe'd like some pizza*, he used to say. Or *why don't we take*

Zoe out for some ice cream? The one who would have given us both a hard time wasn't going to lecture either of us ever again.

I'd share the donuts today, but with Sebastian gone, I'd have to take over the role of stocking his fridge with vegetables to make sure he didn't eat himself into an early grave. Would that be stepping on Maeve's toes? Had anyone ever tried sharing custody of their almost-father-in-law before?

Mr. Clunes led me to his apartment, went straight for the couch after entering, dropped down, and patted the seat beside him as I closed the door behind us. He whistled slightly. Orion cocked his head and looked at me the way a kid might if they were offered a cookie right before supper. He couldn't keep his mouth off my phone, but he knew the "no dogs on the furniture" rule at least.

"Go ahead," I said.

Whether Orion understood the words or the tone, he plunged for the couch, leaped up, and buried his head into Mr. Clunes' side. Orion heaved a huge sigh. I swear, he could have been an emotional support dog for how empathic he was.

I took the armchair. The fabric gave off a faint whiff of pipe tobacco.

Mr. Clunes opened the lid on the donut box and pushed it toward me. "So you know, I told that Detective MacIntosh that you had nothing to do with what happened."

He avoided saying *Sebastian's death* or *Sebastian's murder* the same way someone else might avoid looking at an open wound.

"If Jim Stokley'd still been the one in charge, you never would have been dragged down to the station in the first place. But I couldn't think of anyone who'd have wanted to hurt Seb. And that MacIntosh thought he knew best. What kind of a name is MacIntosh, anyway? That's an apple, not a person." He poked the box again. "Go ahead. Otherwise, I'll eat them all and..."

He swallowed hard. He'd probably been about to say *and Sebastian will chew my ear off when he finds out.*

I took out a chocolate glazed. Chocolate could make everything better, even if only a bit.

I took a bite to buy myself some time to think. I'd been about to walk away before he found me here. Now he'd opened the door. Did that make it less like prying and more like the natural direction of the conversation? It'd be illogical not to take advantage of it, right?

I just had to keep telling myself that and I'd eventually believe it.

The donut bite stuck in my throat like swallowing sawdust, even though it was perfectly moist and cakey. I coughed slightly. "You can't think of anyone? No one at all? Because if you could come up with even a single person, it could help the police stop wasting their time investigating me."

He stared down into the donut box as if even having to make a choice between varieties was too much for him at the moment. He shook his head. "I told Detective Apple to ask Maeve if she could think of anyone. She spent more time with Seb than anyone else, what with them working together and living together. Until a month ago anyway."

A shock like static electricity zapped through me. Maeve had made it sound like everything was perfect with her and Sebastian. "They stopped working together a month ago, or they stopped living together a month ago?"

Mr. Clunes picked up an apple fritter and stared at it the way someone else might stare at a food they didn't recognize. "Living together." His tone was almost absent. "Seb couldn't have run the clinic without Maeve. She's a whiz at keeping things organized."

His voice was filled with affection when he spoke Maeve's name. He'd clearly already started to think of her as family. Her moving out didn't seem to have changed that.

The altered living arrangements explained why I hadn't seen any women's items when I was in Sebastian's house, even though the place looked like a woman had decorated it. It also explained why she hadn't reported him missing before Kat did. She hadn't known he was missing until he didn't show up for work.

Surely the police knew something had gone wrong between them. That should have made Maeve a better suspect than me. My pain was old. Whatever had happened to make Maeve move out had been fresh.

Mr. Clunes was halfway through his fritter. Eating it slowly, as if each bite mattered. As if he wouldn't know what to do next once he'd finished the box.

Only a villain would come right out and ask him if he thought Maeve might have hurt Sebastian, casting doubt on one of the few people he had left. If she turned out to be guilty, the police could do that. But only once there was proof. Not based on suppositions.

If I was going to find out anything more, I needed to tiptoe into it. "Do you think the breakup was permanent?"

He took the last bite. Chewed much longer than was necessary. "I didn't say they were broken up. Couples have bumps. She'd gone back to her parents for a bit until they could work things through. He loved Maeve, and she loved him."

My chest caved in. Mr. Clunes never spoke with that much confidence about my relationship with Sebastian. Sebastian and I fought a lot. Maybe Mr. Clunes saw that and how we were at odds about so many things. Maybe he'd known before I ever did that Sebastian and I wouldn't last.

And maybe Sebastian had cheated because he didn't have the courage to end our relationship any other way. By cheating, he'd made sure I would be the one to break up with him.

So many maybes.

I didn't like maybes.

I took a second donut—a Boston cream. Mr. Clunes

didn't even like filled donuts. The filled donuts were Sebastian's favorites. "What makes you so sure he and Maeve would have worked it out?"

He rested back on the couch and stroked Orion's head. "He left her the house and the business in his will, and he hadn't changed it. He would have changed it if he thought they couldn't patch things up." He sighed. "It was the right thing to do even though they weren't married yet. I certainly didn't need either. I have everything I need for my retirement and then some, plus Seb's life insurance on top of it."

I barely heard the last part.

Maeve *did* have a motive despite claiming she didn't. That opened up so many possibilities. She'd also moved out. Whatever had caused that, she could have been both angry at him for what he'd done and afraid she'd lose her job if they broke up over it. Now she had job security. She owned the veterinary clinic. Once the police released the house, she'd have it, too.

A barrage of questions bubbled up in my mind. Did he know why Maeve moved out? Did he know when Sebastian added Maeve to his will? Did Maeve know she'd been added to Sebastian's will?

I bit my lip to keep from blurting them out with reckless abandon. Patience. Slow and steady.

My phone vibrated in my pocket. When had it started working again?

I couldn't let it ring in case it was Judith. She probably assumed that I'd been able to get my phone fixed with how long I'd been gone.

I pulled it out. The number wasn't familiar, but it could be that lawyer calling back about my grandfather's estate. I probably shouldn't let them go to voicemail.

Mr. Clunes waved for me to take the call. He leaned over the donut box again, examining the remaining options closely. First thing tomorrow, I was buying him a bunch of salads and skinless chicken breasts.

"Hello?" I said.

"Is this Dr. Stephenson?" The woman's voice on the other end of the line was breathless.

I should know that voice. Where had I heard it before? I closed my eyes, but it didn't flash on the back of my eyelids. Being back in Arbor was probably going to have this effect on me a lot as I ran into people I hadn't seen in years. "Speaking."

"I tried calling the after-hours number twice, but it went straight to your voicemail. I had to call the Pet Poison Help Line."

Oh no. I hadn't even thought about that when my phone went down. Since Maeve had allowed me to stay on, my number would have been put on the message for after-hours emergencies. I needed a new phone fast, or to get this one fixed.

Either way, my visit with Mr. Clunes was over for today.

The woman must have been speaking loud enough that he could hear her end of the conversation because he gave me a *go on* hand gesture, letting me know he understood. Orion, on the other hand, took both of us to hoist him off the couch.

I headed for the apartment door. I was about equal distance between my house and the vet clinic. I could get there faster walking than if I tried to head home for the car. "I'll meet you at the clinic," I told the woman on the phone. "Tell me what's going on."

"I called the pet poison line, like I said." The woman's tone was both panicked and imperious. "They told me to give him hydrogen peroxide to make him vomit, so he's been getting sick all over. They said I still needed to get him to my vet right away. That's you."

Not being able to remember who the voice belonged to was like a mosquito bite that wouldn't stop itching no matter how much I scratched. "Do you know what he ate?"

"What does it matter since he's throwing it all up—" Her voice cut off, and then she sighed. "In my car."

I picked up my pace, my flip-flops keeping me from breaking into a jog.

I'd had clients use the Pet Poison Help Line before. The operators didn't usually advise pet owners to administer hydrogen peroxide unless whatever the dog ate was fast-acting and deadly. Inducing vomiting could be dangerous. Some things like batteries could cause serious damage if a dog threw them up, and vomiting always came with the risk of aspiration pneumonia if a dog got stomach fluids into their lungs.

Definitely shouldn't say any of that to an already panicked owner, though. She needed to feel like this was all going to be okay. "Knowing what he ate helps us make sure he won't get sick again. It can also influence the treatment we give him. Does he ever eat your houseplants?"

The sound of tires that had been in the background stopped. She must have reached the clinic ahead of me. "Never. He's not a cow. He's a dog."

She said it in a way that implied that I, as a veterinarian, should have known better. But dogs were omnivores. They would happily snack on fruits and vegetables and roadside plants. Even cats, obligate carnivores, were known for making themselves sick on houseplants.

"Could he have gotten into anything outside? Rat poison? Antifreeze?"

"No. None of that. He tore open the garbage, but he didn't get much. This is all the fault of those pit bull people. They caused this."

Those pit bull people.

I groaned silently. I knew who the voice belonged to now. Madame Mayor.

I turned the last corner before the clinic. She stood outside her car, her dog cradled in her arms and a Bluetooth earpiece over one ear. Her dog was slightly bigger than I'd thought the first time I saw him across the street, maybe ten pounds. He was at least part Papillon based on his silky-looking fur, ears like butterfly wings, and distinctive brown mask contrasting his white body.

This probably hadn't been a poisoning at all. Her dog had probably been a bit tired because of the heat, and she assumed someone had taken revenge on her. Based on what Pastor Keith had told me about threats toward the shelter, there had likely been threats toward the mayor as well. She'd been the one to push for the "dangerous breeds" ban in the first place. That only meant she was paranoid now. It didn't mean anyone had actually poisoned her dog.

The poor little dog. He was the victim of her anger toward "those pit bull people" and how it clouded her judgment.

Since we didn't know what poison he'd hypothetically been given by the people who had issues with his mother, and since he'd already vomited, the best thing I could do for him was lots of fluids and observation. That's the same treatment I would have given him for dehydration or heat stroke anyway. And I'd x-ray his abdomen to make sure he hadn't swallowed any foreign objects. Cover all the bases.

"I'm here now," I said into the phone and disconnected the call.

The mayor's gaze snagged on me. She hugged her little dog closer and scowled. "You? You're the vet?"

Yes, I felt like saying, *and unless you want to drive your sick little guy an hour, I'm the only one you've got.* Instead, I tried to think of how Judith would act, and I smiled consolingly. "I think we got off on the wrong foot earlier. I'm Dr. Zoe Stephenson."

The mayor glanced down at her dog. The sharp angles of her face softened. "Edith Cameron. Can you help him?"

Orion lifted a hind leg to scratch his face and tipped over. Her worry about her dog seemed to have made her blind to Orion's presence. That, or she didn't want to annoy the person who, to her way of thinking, held her dog's life in her hands.

I unlocked the front door of the clinic and punched in the code to silence the alarm. "Bring him inside, and I'll take a look at him. What's his name?"

"Buddy." She kissed the top of his head. "His name's Buddy."

I quickly tucked Orion into one of the empty kennels in the back. He'd howl the whole time, but it was better than him stressing out the mayor by his mere presence. A stressed-out mayor would stress out her dog, and we'd end up in a vicious cycle. It was also better than Orion chewing up something important in the office—like Maeve's chair—and getting me fired.

I examined Buddy, asking Edith a few more questions as I did. He was definitely lackluster. He was awake, but his head drooped. Other than slightly heavy breathing, he seemed fine. His temperature was normal, and his heart sounded good. I took him to the back for x-rays, but everything looked normal there too.

I brought him back to the exam room. "I'd like to keep him and give him some IV fluids."

Edith sniffed. "Certainly you're going to keep him. You don't bring a sick person to the ER because you want to bring them home again without treatment."

This woman required the patience of Job. And I was no Job. Or Esther. Or Stephen. Or any of the people from the Bible who held their tempers and treated everyone with grace and mercy. I was more like Peter, slicing off ears and repenting later.

I gritted my teeth and prayed that it looked like a smile. "With some fluids, I think he'll be fine. If he was going to get worse, we'd have seen it by now."

Edith pressed a hand to her throat and slouched slightly. "Thank you." She glanced back toward the kennel area where Orion's wail mournfully echoed. "I'm sorry about our conversation earlier. With everything that's been going on lately, I'm more sensitive than I otherwise would be. I'm sure you love your dog as much as I love mine. But the law is the law, you know."

The law was only the law because she'd put it in place.

She smiled at me the way she might at a small, precocious child. "I will take your word for it that your dog is a Boxer. He seemed like a Boxer tonight. Everyone knows Boxers are gentle family dogs despite their size."

How magnanimous of her. Good thing she hadn't

decided to institute a size ban instead of a breed ban. The only thing Orion had done differently tonight was topple over while scratching his ear. Maybe that had made him look less threatening than when he was cowering under a table earlier today.

We settled Buddy, and I walked Edith to the door.

She paused with her hand on the handle. "There *is* a plan, isn't there? In case you're arrested for Dr. Clunes' murder? Not to be insensitive, but I hear things as mayor. If Buddy needs to stay for a few days, I want to be sure he'll actually get the care I'm paying for."

Heat burned magma-hot in my chest. *I know you have a gun to your head,* she might as well have said, *but I could really use a Band-Aid right about now.*

Do not react. Don't do it. A happy Madam Mayor would be good for business. An angry one was likely to come up with some sanction to slap on us.

"No need to worry." The smile I gave her was so sweet it could have rotted teeth. "Buddy will be home long before anything like that would happen."

The woman had the gall to actually look relieved.

I locked the door behind her and let out a huge breath.

I freed Orion from his kennel and gave him some extra pets to make up for it. The clinic was almost deathly silent without his screaming. Quiet and empty. All I had left to do was update the file for Buddy, wait for his IV drip to finish, and Orion and I could head home.

I headed to the office and stopped in the doorway.

My breath caught in my throat. If I wanted to poke around into Sebastian's business to find out if something here had gotten him killed, there wouldn't be a better time than now. Edith had made it more obvious than ever that, if I wanted to clear my name, doing so was up to me.

10

The vet clinic's computer systems were new enough that they booted up within seconds. Thank goodness Maeve had given me the password information in case of an emergency visit like tonight's. I updated Buddy's file quickly. When Kat came in tomorrow, she'd send out an invoice.

I rolled the chair closer to the monitor and exited out of the patient files.

All the other file folders on the hard drive were neatly labeled and alphabetized. No one was this organized. Maeve had to be a robot.

I went to the folder marked *Financial Documents* first and skimmed the statements for the past three months. No unexplained expenses, and they were bringing in more than they were spending each month.

I ran a finger down the itemized columns. The amounts they were paying for some of the drugs seemed unusually high. I opened a few client invoices. They weren't charging the clients these escalated prices for medications. The amounts they charged the clients were lower and fairer by far than the last clinic where I'd worked.

Something definitely wasn't right. I clicked over to one of the distributor order forms. Whoever was entering the amounts in the vet clinic's financial statements had routinely added a minimum of ten percent to what the clinic should have been paying for the product. On one medication, that wasn't much, but over an entire order, the amount was significant.

Was this tax fraud? Trying to make their expenses seem higher than they were in order to reduce the amount they were required to pay in taxes?

One of the things Sebastian and I used to fight about was how slippery he was on his taxes. He'd said taxes were too high, and the government didn't deserve that much of our money. He'd wanted to file my taxes for me, and I'd refused to let him.

But that was over five years ago, and he wasn't a complete idiot. You probably needed an accountant to file corporate taxes, and that meant cheating became a lot harder. Plus, I had to imagine the fines for corporate tax evasion were substantial and not worth the risk.

I checked all the financials again. Whoever had done this had only inflated the medication costs, as if they were hoping it wouldn't be noticed the way inflating the costs of everything undoubtedly would have.

Was someone skimming money from the clinic and trying to hide it by making it look like products cost more than they did? Or using the higher prices to hide the fact that they were stealing medications to sell illegally? If they purchased extra but didn't then record that extra amount, it could also explain why the amount paid didn't match up with the recorded inventory.

If one of those scenarios was true, who had been behind it? Sebastian, or Maeve? And why? Did one of them owe money they couldn't pay back, or was this all about greed? Their house *had* been decorated far outside of my budget.

Since Sebastian was dead and Maeve wasn't, it seemed logical that they hadn't been in it together. So either Maeve found out about it and killed him or Sebastian found out about what was going on and Maeve killed him to cover it up.

A chill slithered over my skin. I wrapped my arms around my middle. Reading about murder in books, watching crime shows on TV—none of it compared to thinking that someone you knew had killed another person. That someone you knew had been killed. Whatever Sebastian had done, he didn't deserve to have his final moments be filled with fear and pain. Whoever had done this to him didn't have the right to take his life away like that.

A bad taste rose up at the back of my mouth similar to when I thought about people hunting for sport, only worse. I swallowed hard once, twice. Whoever had killed

Sebastian deserved whatever punishment the court system gave them. Whatever it was wouldn't be enough. Especially if the killer had been Maeve, who was supposed to love him.

A niggling feeling in the back of my mind suggested I was jumping to conclusions by assuming Maeve had been involved at all. Maybe she hadn't known. Maybe Sebastian owed money to someone dangerous, tried to skim funds from the business to pay it back, and when he hadn't paid up fast enough, that person killed him.

Whatever the truth ended up being, Detective MacIntosh needed to see this. He wouldn't still be looking at me if he knew about these discrepancies in the vet clinic's financials. Someone else clearly had a larger and more recent motive than I did.

I clicked the PRINT button, and the printer fired up.

A key ground in the front door's lock.

Was I hearing things?

The lock clicked. Heat, followed by cold, rushed over me. That wasn't my imagination. Someone else was here.

11

I jerked around and barely stopped the chair from sliding across the room. No one else had a reason to be here at this time of night.

A shiver traced down the back of my neck and trailed down my spine. If I'd thought to look for this information, someone else might have as well. His killer might have decided to come and destroy the evidence to cover their tracks. He or she wouldn't have known I'd be here after an emergency call.

They'd waited a long time to dispose of the evidence, though, if it was the killer.

"Hello?" Maeve's voice called out. "Zoe? Kat?"

I tensed. In two of the three scenarios I'd come up with, Maeve murdered Sebastian. I couldn't let her see what I was doing.

But if I closed the file on the computer now, it would stop printing.

I scooted to the office door and leaned casually on the doorframe. The door was partially closed. Hopefully she wouldn't be able to see around me. Or hear the printer.

"It's just me." I forced my voice to sound casual, the way I did when I thought there might be something seriously wrong with an animal, but I wasn't sure yet. My don't-terrify-the-owner voice. "I got an emergency call. What are you doing here?"

That question sounded casual, didn't it? Most people would ask that if someone showed up where they weren't expected to be.

Maeve wiped a strand of hair out of her face. Her hair was pulled back in a French braid, and she wore the type of athletic clothes that women who were proud of their gym habits tended to buy—brand-name and perfectly coordinated.

"I got a notification that the alarm system was disarmed. No one was supposed to be here tonight." She sighed as if she were frustrated with herself. "I forgot that you were on call now."

Without makeup, the circles under her eyes looked like bruises. Her shirt still clung damply to her, as if she'd been on a treadmill, running from demons for a bit too long.

I filled her in on Buddy, talking a little louder than necessary to cover up the sound of the printer. I edged farther and farther from the door as I did. Hopefully Maeve would naturally follow me away.

Halfway through my recounting, Maeve's eyes narrowed, and she tilted her head to the side. "What's that noise?" She plowed forward. "Are you printing something?"

She slid past me and pushed the door open so quickly I could imagine her playing a sport. I stayed out of the way. There wasn't any sense in getting into a shoving match to keep her out.

Besides, if she had murdered Sebastian, it seemed like a smart move to be closer to the exit than she was once she figured out what I'd been doing. By the look of her, she could easily outrun me. I'd need a head start. I eased down and grabbed the end of Orion's leash in case we had to make a break for it and backed up slightly toward the door.

Maeve reappeared in the office doorway, papers from the printer in her hands. She flipped through them. "These are financial statements. I don't understand. I thought you were printing off client information so you could poach our clients for yourself." Her eyebrows lowered, and she shook her head. "None of this will help you do that, will it?"

She could see it wouldn't, so she must not have actually expected an answer. Again.

She brought her gaze back up to my face. "I don't understand."

Was she playing me? She flipped through the papers and glanced back at the computer, where the financial files sat open. Her frown stayed in place.

She honestly had no clue why I would want those files. That seemed to suggest that she hadn't been the one doing something illegal.

She might still have killed Sebastian for doing something illegal, though—but she couldn't understand what I'd want with the evidence?

No, she was smarter than that. She wouldn't be confused about why I'd want evidence that could incriminate her in the crime.

She must have known nothing about it. If that were the case, she needed to take the files to the police.

"I think those files point to something Sebastian was doing that he shouldn't have. Some of the numbers are too high."

Maeve's head moved up and down once, slowly. "That I know. I confronted him about them. That's why I moved back in with my parents. We were business partners. This place was half mine. I had a right to know, and he refused to talk about it. I gave him an ultimatum." Her gaze sharpened again. "But you want them...why?"

My subterfuge had failed me. Maeve would put the pieces together eventually. I might as well lay it out and see how she reacted. "I'm trying to prove I didn't kill Sebastian. No one else seems interested in finding the real killer, so I decided to do it myself."

Maeve rolled her eyes. "And you think that real killer is me. Of course you do."

She actually sounded insulted. Orion gave a hufflesnort from the floor beside me as if he were annoyed by the both of us interrupting his nap. Where was all that spirit he'd shown earlier? He could have at least pretended he'd protect me if Maeve launched herself at me. He must not see her as a threat.

I crossed my arms over my chest. Maeve had thought I killed Sebastian. Being insulted now that the tables were turned was the proverbial pot-and-kettle scenario. "You inherited his half of the business and the house. That gives you a motive that I didn't have. Especially since you just admitted to knowing Sebastian was doing something that could have put your business at risk."

"I'm not a murderer." Maeve said the words slowly, as if I were too dense to understand them if she spoke at a normal pace. "I did the mature thing and put some space between us until he was ready to be honest. If you don't believe me, you can check with my parents. The way the police did. The night Sebastian died, I had supper with them, we all watched a movie, and then I went to bed."

"Sleeping in the same house isn't an alibi. You might have sneaked out. Presumably you don't sleep in the same room as your parents."

Maeve shot me a look that said *How did you graduate if you're this stupid?* "Of course not. But my parents have an alarm system that logs every time the system is armed or disarmed and every time a door or window opens. They armed the house before we sat down to watch the movie, and the alarm company logs can prove nothing was opened or disarmed until the next morning. Did you never wonder why the police weren't looking at me as a suspect?"

I had wondered. I'd thought it had to do with the bad blood between Sebastian and me. And with the fact that Maeve was more professional than I was. Not to mention that she didn't have a parent in prison. She could have talked her way out of being a suspect. I wasn't nearly that smooth.

"No one in Arbor has a security system. Most people don't lock their doors." The words sounded like petty heel-dragging even to me, but it wasn't like I could take them back.

"No one who grew up in a small town locks their doors." Maeve still spoke more slowly than was necessary. "My parents moved here from Detroit to be closer to me when Sebastian and I moved here. The first thing they did was add a security system to their house." Her words ended on a huff. "And given what happened to Sebastian, it's clear they were right to be worried. Arbor hasn't proven itself to be safe. Sales of alarm systems are sure to go up now if people know what's good for them."

A seed of anger took root in my stomach, unfurling up into my chest. Arbor was the most beautiful town in existence. If she didn't like it here, she and her parents could go back to Detroit or some other big, ugly city.

But she did have a point. The landscape of small towns started changing during the last few years. A lot of people had wanted out of the cities and had moved to more rural areas. The culture of locked doors and security systems no doubt came with them. The cell phone repair shop had a whole wall of security systems. That wouldn't be the case if they weren't selling.

"Why didn't you say all that the other day when I said spouses are the most likely suspect in a murder?"

"It was none of your business, and I didn't owe you an explanation, now did I?" Her voice was almost as haughty as Madam Mayor Edith's.

Unfortunately, if Maeve was telling the truth, she couldn't have killed Sebastian. That brought the options down to one—Sebastian had been doing something involving controlled medications, and it got him killed.

My brain jumped around looking for any other explanation. He'd cheated on me, yes, but he still had other standards. He couldn't have been selling drugs. Could he? "Why not take the financial discrepancies to the police, then? Since you claim to have nothing to hide."

Maeve drew in a breath and dropped the papers on the front desk. They hit with a thwap. "They didn't seem pertinent. I was sure you killed Sebastian. The only reason I let you work here was so I could keep an eye on you. I figured you'd eventually slip up and say something that would prove you were guilty."

I snorted. I shouldn't have been surprised. She'd said as much when she almost refused to hire me.

A tight little knot formed at the bottom of my throat. It would have been nice, though, if someone I wasn't related to—other than Mr. Clunes—had at least considered I might not be capable of murder, either.

I gave myself a mental shake. It was fine. I didn't need Maeve or anyone else in this town to like me. All that mattered was clearing my name. And Judith, my parents, and Mr. Clunes believed in my innocence. They were the ones who mattered.

I picked up the papers. "If *you* didn't kill Sebastian, and *I* didn't kill Sebastian, then the police need to see these."

"I suppose you're right." Maeve squished her lips together as if the admission tasted bad. "But we can't take your dog, and the police station is too far to walk."

I leaned back and peeked out the window. Maeve had apparently walked or run here from wherever she'd been as well. That made it seem like she was being honest and not simply looking for a way to avoid going to the police.

Still, I wasn't going to let her out of my sight until this was done. "My house is in walking distance. We can drop Orion off and take my car."

***

Maeve leaned across the console of my car and looked at the flashing low-fuel light on my dashboard. "You know, it's not more expensive to keep the top half full than the bottom half."

That bossy attitude probably helped the veterinary clinic run well, but this was *my* car. "We have enough to get there."

Maeve shrugged and gave a little huff. "Fine. Your choice. But you realize I won't be the one walking to the gas station to buy a gas can, don't you?"

I clenched my teeth. Giving in was better than listening to her for the rest of the drive. I threw on my clicker and made a last-second turn into the gas station we were about to drive past.

A handwritten sign on an orange piece of paper flapped in the wind as we pulled up to the pump. Great. They were probably out of gas, and I'd have given in to Maeve for nothing.

No Diesel, the sign read.

Thank goodness.

I quickly filled my car up, paid, and climbed back in.

Maeve held an uncapped bottle of hand sanitizer upside down, as if she expected me to hold out my hands like a compliant child. Part of me wanted to sit on my hands to make a point, but that would have made it hard to drive.

Maeve wiggled the bottle slightly. "You never know how many people have touched the pump before you."

Had Sebastian actually liked this about her? This need to control everything?

But she wasn't going to let this go until I gave in. Somehow, it didn't seem worth the battle. I held out my hands, and she dropped a perfect quarter-size dollop into it. "Happy now?"

Maeve's gaze slid away from mine. She recapped the bottle and tucked it back into her purse. "No." Her words were almost too soft to hear over the blasting air conditioner. "But thank you."

What in the world? That definitely hadn't been the reaction I'd been expecting. I'd thought she would give me a patronizing *Yes, thank you.*

I'd assumed Maeve was just bossy. Maybe I'd misjudged her. Maybe she was more like me. She might need to control things to deal with anxiety she felt when she could see potential problems coming. When enough people let you down, it was hard to trust someone else to get things right without your supervision and direction. When enough bad things happened, overpreparing could be a way to feel like you could cope with whatever came next.

According to the counselor I'd seen as a teenager, part of my desire to be prepared by carrying everything I could possibly need with me had to do with the fact that I rarely had what I needed when I was little. And then I'd been ripped out of my home by child services without a chance to even collect what few belongings I did have. I didn't know Maeve well enough to know if she might have a similar defining experience in her past. I probably shouldn't be so hard on her.

Maeve glanced over at me and raised her eyebrows. "Are we going to sit here all night? I have other things to do."

Or maybe she was just bossy.

We drove in silence the rest of the way to the police station. My hands were clenched around the wheel so tightly they ached. Every time Maeve drew a deep breath, I tensed, waiting for another criticism. God certainly had a sense of humor. I'd wanted to work on my temper, so he'd put me with someone who made me want to throw bricks through glass windows simply to watch them shatter.

Maeve drummed her fingers on the file folder of the financials I'd printed out as if she needed an outlet, too.

I parallel parked while Maeve gave me instructions on how to do it better, and she wouldn't take *no* for an answer when the woman at the front desk tried to tell us that Detective MacIntosh was busy but that she could take the papers for us.

Maeve gave her a look that could have melted stone. "Detective MacIntosh told me that I should come to him at any time if I thought of something related to my fiancé's murder. I have. Don't you think he'd want to know I was here?"

The woman behind the desk looked as if she appreciated Maeve's tone about as much as I had. But she did dial a number on her phone.

She hung up the receiver and pointed at the chairs along the wall. There were only four, and they weren't bolted to the floor. I'd always imagined they would be, so that they couldn't be thrown at the plexiglass that separated the desk clerk from the waiting area.

"Take a seat." Her voice was almost eerily calm. They must train police officers and their adjuvants how to not allow people to get to you. "He'll be right out."

Detective MacIntosh entered the lobby from a side door. His gaze hit me and then Maeve. The expression that passed over his face made me think he suspected we'd been brought down to the station for getting into a brawl with each other rather than that we'd come here willingly and together.

Maeve rose to her feet and brushed her shorts off the same way she would a skirt. She held the file folder out to him. "We have information about the case."

She didn't have to say which case. Arbor wasn't a town where people were often murdered. Sebastian's case was probably the only open murder investigation at present.

Detective MacIntosh didn't take the file from her. "If you'd both come with me, I'd like to ask you a few questions. There's an empty room this way."

The back of my throat dried out. He shouldn't need to put us in a room. Suspects went into rooms. We were only dropping off information. This couldn't possibly make me end up looking even more guilty, could it?

"It doesn't look like anyone will disturb us if we stay right here." Maeve gestured at the empty lobby. "Last time you asked me to join you in a room, I ended up staying there for twice the amount of time it should have taken."

I wrestled down a smirk. It was like she'd read my mind.

Detective MacIntosh's gaze slipped in my direction, and he narrowed his eyes as if he could feel my desired smirk. I mentally stuck my tongue out at him and blew a raspberry. Had Maeve not been there, I might have done it for real, but then I'd have had to listen to how immature I was all the way home.

She held out the file folder the same way she'd held out the hand sanitizer bottle to me earlier, and Detective MacIntosh took it. Which was kind of unfortunate. I'd have loved to see her shake it at him in a *What are you waiting for?* way.

Maeve quickly explained what he'd find inside.

He opened the folder and glanced at it. "Were you two lying to me about not knowing each other prior to Sebastian's death?"

His words were casual, as if it'd only occurred to him now. Which meant he'd most likely considered it from the beginning. I would have if I were on the outside looking in. He knew Sebastian had cheated on me, and someone who had cheated once was more likely to cheat again. He also knew that Maeve had moved out. Whatever reason she gave, he'd suspect her of lying because the police always seemed to assume people were lying—if TV shows could be trusted, at least.

The way he was trying to act casual seemed like he might suspect us of conspiring to kill Sebastian if we'd found out he cheated on us both. Two women cheated on by the same man taking revenge was the theme of enough country music songs to be practically a cliché.

My chest went tight and hot. Either way, this was supposed to help clear my name, not drag Maeve down with me if she were innocent, too. "You don't have to believe us, but you'll be wasting even more time if you try to find a link between us. We met the same day you told us Sebastian was dead. We didn't have to bring this to you. We did it because we both want the truth, and we've put aside our differences long enough to get it."

The look he gave me said he thought the more likely reason was because we wanted to throw him off our trail.

He shifted his gaze to Maeve. "Are you willing to give me access to all your financials, both business and personal?"

Maeve arched one eyebrow. "I wouldn't have come otherwise."

He whapped the file folder closed. "I'll look into it, but I expect you both to be available for questioning. At my convenience. For however long it takes."

I clenched my teeth and opened my mouth to tell him exactly what he could do with his demands, but Maeve laid a hand on my arm.

"As long as you show proper respect for us and our grief," she said. "We've lost someone, and we deserve some common decency. We also have jobs we can't abandon at your whims."

Her hand on my arm drew my gaze and trapped it there like fruit flies into vinegar. Pressure built at the back of my eyes, and I blinked rapidly. She'd stuck up for me. Not that Maeve probably did it for me. She was sticking up for herself, too... but still.

"Yes, ma'am." Detective MacIntosh's voice held only a touch of sarcasm. He turned around and headed back toward the door he'd come out of. "Sebastian sure did have a type."

The words were soft enough that it wasn't clear whether he'd intended for us to hear him or not.

A type? I turned to face Maeve. Her lips twitched spastically, as if she wanted to grin but didn't want to give Detective MacIntosh the satisfaction if he looked back.

A laugh built in my chest, and I bit my bottom lip and nudged Maeve toward the door.

As soon as the door closed behind us, my giggle broke loose. "He's awful. I'm sure he was implying we're both..." The word he'd probably been thinking was the term used for female dogs.

One side of Maeve's lips quirked up. "Strong and determined?"

I snorted. "Yeah, I'm sure that was it."

12

"If you had to guess, what would you say Sebastian was up to?" I swiveled my stool around from the FIV screening test I'd been running. I had a few minutes to wait for the results. I leaned back a bit so I could see Maeve in the office. "When you confronted him, what did you think he'd say?"

Kat glanced over at me and held a finger up to her lips, phone pressed tightly to her ear. She'd been on hold, waiting for the pharmaceutical rep for fifteen minutes now. She should have been glad for a break from the muzak.

I rolled the stool until I was perched in the office door, closer to Maeve.

Maeve didn't turn away from the computer screen. "We've passed the paperwork along to the detective.

Don't you have better things to worry about? Like repairing your phone?"

She had a point. My cell phone had refused to turn on for the last two days.

"It's not like I'm procrastinating on purpose." I pointed to the clock on the wall. "By the time I'm done here every day, the repair place is closed. I changed the emergency message on the machine to Judith's cell number so I'm not missing any important calls."

Except the lawyer. I hadn't been able to return the call to the lawyer about the inheritance. An internet search hadn't turned up the firm because I didn't know what state it was located in. My grandfather had moved around a lot. Until I could get the information off my phone, I was out of luck.

Maeve made an excuses-excuses noise. "You're going to look guilty if Detective MacIntosh calls and your phone always sends him immediately to voicemail."

Why did she always have to be right? It was an extremely annoying quality. "I'll go first thing on Saturday. In the meantime, I don't see why we can't at least talk about possible reasons Sebastian might have been fudging the financials. I don't want to hang all my hopes on Detective MacIntosh."

"Can we not talk about it?" Kat asked from behind me. "Please?"

I spun the stool around. Her face had taken on a gray-green cast.

"It's not something we need to worry about." She blurted out the words. "And it's morbid. I can't stand it."

Maybe I was being insensitive. I'd once been closer to Sebastian, but I hadn't seen him in five years. Maeve had been his fiancée, and Kat had worked with him every day. They both had to be hurting now more than I was.

"You're outvoted," Maeve said.

I'd drop the subject out of respect for them, but that didn't mean I had to let her have the last word. "I thought you said this wasn't a democracy."

Kat giggled. She hadn't gotten herself back under control by the time the rep finally came on the phone.

***

I got up early on Saturday, walked Orion, and headed downtown. The cell phone repair shop was supposed to be open Saturday mornings, assuming I remembered the sign correctly.

This time, I was going to camp out in front of the shop and not leave until someone showed up.

The streets were mostly empty. The few people I met along the way stayed on my side of the road, confirming that the people I'd passed before had crossed the street to avoid Orion. The ice cream shop was still closed. Next door, True Loaf Bakery had a short line out the door, and an employee in an apron maneuvered around them, wiping down the outdoor tables. The scents of freshly brewed coffee, yeast, and sugar left my mouth watering.

I glanced down at my travel mug. Not a mocha latte, but it'd have to do. My budget didn't allow for luxuries right now. No way was I going to be like Tonya, buying the wants when we couldn't even afford the needs.

A brick propped open the repair store's door. I strode inside. The shop smelled slightly musty, like warm plastic and old cardboard. The air didn't move at all, as if the place didn't even have air conditioning. It'd be like a sweat box come July if it didn't.

The man behind the counter had rusty brown hair and a graying beard that reached partway down his chest. He must have heard me coming because he looked up from something with wires that he was working on. "I'm Jack. What can I help you with?"

I held up my paperweight of a cell phone. "It had a run-in with my dog."

He grinned like a kid on Christmas morning. "Give it here, and I'll see what I can do."

The way he looked at my cell phone, you would have thought I'd offered him a new video game.

I wandered around the small display area. Just like I'd thought, the new phones were out of my price range, unless I wanted to get stuck with a payment plan that cost me more in the long run. That'd be an absolute last resort if my phone couldn't be fixed.

I veered away from the phones, ear buds, cases, and other accessories so I wouldn't be tempted. It was always too easy to justify purchases as necessary, even when they really weren't.

The only other things to look at in the shop were the security systems. He offered three different options, ranging from self-monitored to Fort Knox. As the one place in town where you could buy a security system, this must have been where Maeve's parents got theirs.

I'd linked my fate with Maeve's in a sense by going with her to the police station, but that didn't necessarily mean I should take her story at face value. She hadn't planned to take the financial information to the police. I'd had to press her on it. Since I was here, I might as well check out her story. If she were telling the truth, I could cross at least one person off my list.

I glanced back over my shoulder to where Jack hunched over my phone, the tip of his tongue sticking out between his teeth.

"Hey." I tried to keep my voice off-the-cuff. "Were you the one who installed the security system for the Stokes? I work with their daughter, Maeve, and I was considering getting the same model they have."

Not a complete lie. I might one day want a security system. Just not any day soon.

Jack made an affirmative noise but didn't look up. "That was me. They come from Detroit, so they got the top-of-the-line system."

I moved down the wall until I reached the high-end system. The specs touted lots of features that sounded like gobbledygook to me. "Does this system log entries and exits so that I could see whenever my doors or windows are opened?"

"Yes, ma'am."

That part of Maeve's story matched with the truth at least. "Is there any way around it? I know that sometimes systems can be hacked or circumvented, and there's not much point in having a system if that can happen."

My phone was in pieces in front of him. Jitters raced through me like this was my tenth cup of coffee instead of my first. What would I do if he couldn't repair it?

He started reassembling my phone with the same ease as a soldier would disassemble, clean, and reassemble a rifle. "I can't never say never, but getting around the system would take more skills than anyone I know. You'd have to be some kind of professional spy for the government or something." He gave me a toothy grin and stroked his beard. "And if you're looking to keep the government out of your house, I don't think a security system's gonna do it."

No, probably not. So Maeve had been telling the truth. It seemed unlikely she had a double life as a CIA operative. And it seemed like a stretch to believe that her parents would have taken the risk of lying about her being with them when the police could check their alarm system logs.

Maeve hadn't killed Sebastian.

I drew in a deep breath, and the aching sensation in my jaw eased. How long had I been tensed up without realizing it?

Maeve's innocence should have been a bad thing,

really. If she'd killed Sebastian, I was off the hook. If she hadn't, the killer was still running around loose, and I had only a vague idea of where to look next. When any other leads dried up, and I still looked like the best option, the police might pin it on me just to have the case closed and keep the public happy. The local paper already had a front-page article this week asking if Arbor was getting more dangerous and criticizing the police for not keeping the public safe.

All things considered, I should have felt disappointed to learn Maeve couldn't have done it. Was I actually starting to like her? And that was why I felt like I wasn't bracing for impact anymore now that I knew she couldn't have killed Sebastian?

Not possible. Not someone that bossy and prissy.

But she did run a good clinic. She booked enough time for appointments, rather than trying to squeeze in too many patients to make extra money. She was fair with her prices. And yesterday I'd even overheard her working out a payment plan with an elderly woman so that she could get the care her cat needed.

Jack rose to his feet and came around the front of his work table. I tilted my head back to look at him. Sitting down, he'd looked like anyone else. Standing up, he was basketball-player tall.

He handed my phone back. "You ever seen those cars where pieces are held on by duct tape, or they got cardboard over a window?"

My phone's home screen once again showed the

time. I pocketed my phone and pulled out my wallet. "Yes."

"That's your phone. It'll work, but it's not going to work like it used to. And I can't make you any guarantees for how long it'll last. You're gonna want to get a new one soon."

I heaved a sigh. Easier said than done. "How much do I owe you?"

He wrote up a receipt for me. "If you buy a new phone from me, I'll take this off the price. See anything you want more info on for the security systems?"

Based on the prices listed under them, they were even further outside the realm of possibility than a new phone was. "Maybe later. I share a house with my sister, and I couldn't make that decision without her."

He pulled gently on his beard. "Who's your sister?"

"Judith Dawson. She works at the animal shelter."

"Oh yeah? I know Judith. Why don't you talk it over with her?" He shrugged. "You know where to find me if you change your mind. Judith did some window shopping on the security stuff, too, not long ago. With all the death threats she was getting over that pit bull the shelter wouldn't give back, she might feel safer if you had one."

Chills ran down both my arms, sending goosebumps scurrying in their wake. Pastor Keith had mentioned threats against the shelter. No one, including Judith, had told me she'd personally received death threats. My stomach churned uncomfortably, and I swallowed hard.

Jack held the credit card terminal out to me. "You're looking at me like I just shone a flashlight straight in your eyes. Didn't no one tell you 'bout the threats?"

I shook my head and tapped my card on the screen. "I knew about the ones against the shelter. Just not that someone threatened Judith personally."

He tore off the credit card receipt, and I took it numbly.

"I'm sure Judith didn't want to scare you now it's past. She turned them emails and voicemails over to the police like I told her to. Then Dr. Clunes proved that dog was pure pittie, and the owner was lying when he said he wasn't. Threats and protests stopped after that, I heard. Ain't no one gonna keep backing a proven liar."

I should have put it all together when Pastor Keith said someone performed a DNA test on the pit bull to prove his breed. The most obvious candidate for running that test would have been Sebastian, the local vet. Which meant he'd probably received death threats, too.

My legs went weak and brittle, like they were going to snap off at the knees if I tried to move. I touched a hand to Jack's work table for support.

And now Sebastian was dead. Judith had been in an accident. And the mayor who advocated for the dangerous breed ban in the first place had her own dog poisoned.

All three people who'd been involved with seizing and re-homing the pit bull had suffered in some way.

That all seemed like too much of a pattern to be a coincidence.

And if I was right, Judith might still be in danger.

13

A car I didn't recognize was parked outside the house when I got back. Judith hadn't mentioned anyone would be stopping by today.

My heart kicked faster in my chest, and my whole body shook, as if I hadn't eaten in days.

I sucked in a deep breath. Whoever was here likely wasn't a danger. Someone would have to be bold to the point of stupid to attack Judith in our house during the day. If snooping were an Olympic sport, the neighbors in Arbor would take the gold medal every year.

Besides, Orion was inside. He didn't have an ounce of aggressiveness in his blood, but he did have what many dogs who'd been abused had—a trigger button. While they wouldn't act if someone threatened them, they would protect people who'd finally made them feel safe. Hopefully that would include Judith.

I burst through the door, kicked off my flip flops, and headed for her room. "Jude!"

Orion streaked out of the kitchen, his tail wagging in circles, tongue lolling.

My heartbeat slowed back to normal. Orion wouldn't look like that if Judith were in danger.

"In here," Judith's voice called from the kitchen.

What sounded like a man's voice said something, but I couldn't catch the words.

Judith sat in her wheelchair next to the breakfast nook table, still in her pajamas. A man with streaks of gray in his hair and dressed in an animal control uniform sat across from her. They had mugs in front of both of them, and a bag from True Loaf Bakery rested in the center of the table.

He got to his feet. "Bob Bremnes. I work with Judith. And you must be Zoe."

Judith had mentioned a Bob more than once, but from the way she talked about him, I'd thought he was younger. I'd even teased her a couple times about having a crush on him with how often he'd come up. Probably not appropriate anymore, since he had to be a good decade older than us.

He motioned back at a bag on the table. "I brought you one, too. An everything bagel with strawberry cream cheese. Judith said that's your favorite."

My stomach rumbled. I had skipped breakfast. And I couldn't exactly light into Judith over why she hadn't told me about the threats now that Bob was here.

I took a seat. "Thank you. It was nice of you to think of me."

Bob grinned. The pair went back to chatting about who'd been adopted from the shelter in the past week and Judith's plans for the fall fundraiser.

My mind wouldn't focus on any of it, stuck on the hamster wheel of *death threats, death threats, death threats*. I methodically ate my bagel, barely tasting it.

Bob glanced between me and Judith in a way that said he'd noticed I wasn't taking part in the conversation. He slapped his hands on the top of his thighs. "Well, I better get back to the shelter. Never know when a call will come in." He put a hand on Judith's shoulder as he walked by. "I'll see you next Saturday."

Judith thanked him for coming. Orion followed him, trying to lick Bob's hand the whole way. Orion was an impeccable judge of character.

The door clicked shut behind him. Orion wandered back in and dropped by Judith's chair. What a traitor.

Judith gave me a look that said *I'm waiting*. Somehow it also carried the implication that I'd better have a good reason for being inhospitable with her friend.

But she didn't get to eyeball me that way. This time she was the one who was in trouble.

"Why didn't you tell me about the death threats?" I spat the words out. Our mom always preferred the gentle approach, something about the Bible saying that a gentle word turns away wrath. But how were you supposed to make something like death threats sound gentle?

Judith pulled a giant chocolate chip muffin from the bag, placed it on her plate, and nudged it in my direction. Like that was supposed to make what she'd done alright. "I told you about the threats."

"You told me the shelter received threats. I assumed people were threatening to shut you down somehow, or to break in and steal the dog, or to vandalize the building." I shoved the plate back toward her. "You didn't say *death threats*. You didn't say *you* got death threats. That's different, and you know it."

I wanted to shake her and yell and tell her she needed to take this seriously. My whole body was tight with the need.

Judith sat quietly with her hands folded on the table. Waiting. That'd been her tactic since early in our life together. We'd never had the shouting matches that some sisters did because you couldn't fight with someone who didn't fight back. Judith just waited out my anger.

That was probably my fault. I'd been the volatile, loud, needy child, and Judith had to find a way to live with my temper. Her quiet calm ended up being the thing I usually needed the most.

Anger is often fear in disguise, a voice in my head that sounded suspiciously like my counselor said.

Fear that I wouldn't be allowed to keep living with my dad. Fear that he'd decide he didn't want me. Fear that someone would take control away from me. Fear of embarrassment. So much fear.

I sucked in a deep breath, and my chest deflated.

I didn't need a professional to tell me why I was angry now.

But I didn't need to hide behind that anger with Judith. I didn't need to push her away to protect myself. She was one of my safe people.

"What if I lost you, too? I know I shouldn't yell at you because I'm scared, but I can't lose you."

"No one said fear was rational." Judith touched a knuckle to the edge of the plate, moving it back in my direction the tiniest fraction. "I'm sorry, too. I should have told you."

I hunched down into the chair. Part of me wanted to ignore the muffin. But it was chocolate chip. I slid it the rest of the way toward me, effectively accepting her peace offering. "Did you not trust me enough to tell me all of it?"

Judith folded the bag into halves, then into quarters. She stared hard at it. "I knew it would blow over. I didn't want you to overreact. You already sounded stressed whenever I called."

I held back a flinch. Judith had been dealing with all of this at the same time as I'd been trying to hide the situation surrounding my last job. I'd known what Judith would say if she found out. She'd have been disappointed in me. Part of my stress had come from hiding it from her. I'd been so busy finding ways to withhold the truth without actually lying that I hadn't noticed Judith was keeping something from me as well.

A failure. That's what I was. A failure as a big sister. Too focused on myself to notice that Judith needed me. She was a terrible liar. The only thing that could explain her getting away with it was my self-absorption.

I blew out a breath. I couldn't fix the past. What I could do was be more honest with Judith going forward. "I think it might not have blown over."

Judith's eyebrows drew down. "I haven't gotten any threats in weeks. Neither has the shelter."

Always-think-the-best Judith. She couldn't think like a murderer even if she tried. If I were going to hurt someone, I'd make sure I stopped threatening them well before. That way I could claim I'd moved on if I was questioned later. "I think your accident might not have been an accident." The words physically hurt. Judith shouldn't have to be afraid, but sometimes fear served a purpose in keeping us safe. "Do you think someone might have been angry enough to follow through on one of those threats? Against both you and Sebastian?"

Judith sucked in a breath like I'd hit her in the stomach instead of asking her a question. She shook her head, then nodded. "I don't know. Maybe. Yes. Some of the threats were..." She blinked hard, but tears slid out. She grabbed the napkin that had come with my bagel and wiped her cheeks. "We were following the law. We didn't even agree with it. Sebastian and I planned to argue for the repeal of the ban at the next council meeting."

That turned things on their head. If she and Sebastian were advocating for what the threat-makers wanted, they'd have no reason to hurt either of them. "Would the dog's owner or anyone else on his side have known that?"

Judith had slumped in her wheelchair, the grown-up version of the way a child might pull the covers over their head after a nightmare. "Only the council members knew. After the protesting at the shelter, we didn't want the pro-pit bull crowd turning up with nasty signs or trying to bully the councilors."

"Did you ever speak out against the ban beforehand? Or tell anyone you didn't agree with it?"

Judith licked her lips as if she were trying to smooth the way for the words to come out. "No, we kept it private. I wanted to go through the proper channels. Sebastian didn't want it to look like we were intimidated by them or caving to their pressure. We weren't trying to change the law because they threatened us. We were doing it because we didn't want to have to enforce a law we didn't agree with in the future."

That was another lesson our parents taught us. The only reason to break the law was if the law required you to go against what the Bible said. Otherwise, whether you liked it or not, you followed the law. My parents took it so seriously that they didn't even speed or jaywalk.

Judith's attempt to show proper respect to those in authority, and Sebastian's refusal to be seen bending to the will of bullies, could have put the threat-makers in a position where they felt like they needed to escalate things to get their way.

I took Judith's hand. Her fingers might have had ice water rather than blood running through her veins for how cold they were. "If the threat-makers saw the ban coming up on the docket, do you think they might have assumed you and Sebastian would be arguing on the side of continuing or even strengthening the ban?"

"Yes." The word came out in a whisper.

Crap. Why couldn't this have been the time when I was wrong? Looking paranoid or silly would have been so much better than being right.

And whoever was behind this hadn't stopped with the attempt on Judith's life. They'd continued attacking the people they blamed for what had happened. Maybe they'd think Judith's broken leg was punishment enough. Or maybe they were waiting for a chance to finish what they started.

Prickles traced their way up my back and down over my arms. My half-finished muffin sat on my plate, but my throat was too tight to get even a crumb more down. "Did they find any of the people behind the threats?"

One side of Judith's mouth tipped up even though tears still sneaked from her eyes. "They didn't ever sign them or leave a name on voicemail. The police told me the emails were from free accounts that didn't have a name attached to them, and the calls came from public locations. And all the IP addresses showed was which town they were from. Some from here, some from outside Arbor."

How could people from Arbor have sunk to that level? This town had always seemed to love animals more than most. There was even a group that took care of the feral cat colony on the west end of town, trapping every new cat who showed up and making sure it was spayed and neutered.

Then again, the people issuing the threats probably saw themselves as the true animal lovers because they didn't discriminate against any animal, regardless of breed.

A frustrated scream built inside my chest. I pushed it back down. Breathe in for four beats, hold for four. Breath out for four beats, hold for four. The box breathing made me feel silly, but society frowned on adults throwing tantrums. Which was a pity. Sometimes a good tantrum might make me feel a lot better. Scream it all out like opening a pressure release valve.

Losing your temper hasn't ever got you anywhere, I reminded myself. *Work the problem instead.*

I knew how to solve problems. When I was assessing an animal, I started with what we knew. What did we know here?

We didn't have the names of all the threat-makers, but we did know for sure one person who'd been involved. "Did the pit bull's owner seem as angry as all the others? Was he a ringleader for it?"

Judith shivered. "He may have wanted revenge on us whether we wanted to change the law or not. We didn't just take his dog. We took away his income. It turned out he was breeding and selling purebred puppies for over $2000 apiece. Plus whatever he got from stud fees on the dog."

"He had a second pit bull?"

Judith nodded. "She was shipped to a shelter out of town, too. We tried to keep it quiet for obvious reasons."

Greed served as a motive for a lot of crimes, murder not least among them.

Judith turned her gaze to mine. Her pupils were so big that her brown eyes looked almost black. "You actually think someone tried to kill me?"

Lies popped to my lips. A little lie and Judith would feel better. *It was probably an accident. A coincidence. You're perfectly safe.*

But Judith wasn't some doll I could control. She wasn't my child, either, as our mom loved to remind me growing up. I'd often tried to mother and shelter Judith. Accepting the role of sister instead hadn't come easily when I'd been mothering Tonya for so long.

"I think we need to consider it." I got up and poured us both another cup of coffee. "Tell me again everything you remember about the accident."

Again might have been too generous to myself. When I got the call about Judith, I'd only asked for the bare details. All I'd cared about—all that had seemed important at the time—was that she was alive and was going to be okay.

"There's not much to tell. I came down that hill by the river, on my way to the council meeting." Judith cradled her mug in her hands. "When I pressed my foot on the brakes to slow down for the curve at the bottom, nothing happened."

The forbidden road, we'd once called it. Forbidden to us by our parents when we first got our learner's permits, even though it was the fastest route from one side of town to the other. We had to take the route through town that took twice as long thanks to all the stop signs, street lights, and one-way streets, on penalty of losing our car privileges for a month if we disobeyed. My parents were too afraid that one of us would become the third wooden cross marking that particular hill and curve. As adults, we took that road all the time. It was really only dangerous if you were driving too fast or the road was covered in snow and ice.

Or your brakes gave out.

"I don't remember anything after that." Judith's voice didn't shake. It was calm, like she was talking about something she'd seen in a movie rather than something she'd experienced. "Ryan told me that it was lucky Keith was behind me, headed to the council meeting, too, and saw me lose control of the car. Apparently, my car hit a tree, and he got me out before it caught fire."

My skin felt uncomfortably tight. Pastor Keith of the

Borrowed Shaver had saved Judith's life. I needed to figure out some way to thank him. How ungrateful must I have seemed that I hadn't even said anything to him about what he'd done? Hopefully he realized I hadn't known before now. I needed to make sure he knew. I needed to make it right.

The idea threatened to hijack my brain. A plan to fix this. That's what I needed, and then I could go back to dealing with Judith's safety.

I could bake Pastor Keith a batch of cookies. I'd write him a long thank-you note and explain that I'd only found out today.

The spiraling sensation inside my chest calmed slightly. I put a mental checkmark beside fixing my unintentional mistake.

My chest grew heavy again. If only protecting Judith would be so easy. "Did Detective MacIntosh tell you why your brakes failed?"

Judith clasped her hands in her lap. Tightly. "My braking system lost fluid pressure due to a leak."

She repeated the words carefully, as if making sure she got them all right. She sounded like someone trying to repeat a phrase in a foreign language. Our dad was a great man, but he hadn't been very good at fixing things, which meant neither of us had been taught anything about vehicles beyond where to take our car for repairs.

I understood only enough to know her brakes wouldn't work because the fluid that made them work was gone. "What caused the leak? Did they say?"

Judith shrugged, holding her shoulders at the top a little longer than necessary. "The crime scene techs had a mechanic look at it. They couldn't be sure. At the time, they thought wear and tear seemed more likely than sabotage."

Convincing them to reopen the investigation would take some work. Step one—prove the man whose pit bull was seized, or someone close to him, was angry enough to retaliate. "What was the name of the pit bull's owner?"

"Tim Gilpin. Why?"

"I'm going to go talk to him."

14

Judith's mouth formed a giant "O." "You want to go talk to the man you spent the last half hour convincing me probably cut my brakes and killed Sebastian? You should leave that up to the police."

"No way is Detective MacIntosh going to listen to me if I bring this theory to him. Not without better proof. Not so soon after bringing him the financial stuff from the clinic. He'll think I'm throwing out every possible idea to deflect suspicion from myself."

I could almost hear him now. *Didn't you just tell me that Sebastian might have been killed because of something with his business? Can't make up your mind? That's fishy. Did you and your sister kill Sebastian together?*

He might not actually say *that's fishy*, but I wouldn't put it past him to suggest Judith had been in on Sebastian's murder. It did sound like he liked her better than me, though, so maybe he wouldn't try to drag her into it.

I held up my hands in a hear-me-out gesture. "Detective MacIntosh has the resources to look into what financial trouble Sebastian might have been in. He can get his bank records and phone records. He can pull the log from Sebastian's GPS, if he had one. I have no way to follow up on any of that. But I can talk to Tim Gilpin without making him suspicious. I'll tell him I'm there to give him a final update on his dogs. He might let something slip that he wouldn't around the police."

Judith's concerned crinkle was back between her eyes. "Is that safe?"

My chest tightened. No way could I fend off Gilpin if he decided to attack me. I couldn't even open a jar of pasta sauce without help. Prison didn't seem so bad if the alternative was death.

But I couldn't give up and do nothing. The stress would build up inside me until it crushed my lungs and left me unable to breathe.

Besides, he'd need a better reason than me showing up at his door to want to kill me. I hadn't been involved in taking his dogs. I wasn't a threat to him at all.

I worried my bottom lip with my teeth. Judith's downturned lips said she wasn't going to buy any of that. "Then we need to make it safer. I won't go inside his house. He won't do anything if there are witnesses."

"And you'll text me every ten minutes. You miss by even a minute and I'm calling the police."

Detective MacIntosh would have a field day if she did that. Impeding an investigation. Witness tampering. Whatever he thought might stick. He'd be sure to come up with some excuse to arrest me.

I crossed my heart. "Every ten minutes. Promise."

Now all I needed to do was get Tim Gilpin's address from the shelter's files.

***

Bob Bremnes didn't even question me when I showed up at the shelter and said I needed to look at some of the files. As the only local vet, apparently I had unrestricted access because they were all considered my patients. The only hold-up was when a woman brought in a stray cat and her four kittens that she'd been feeding for a week until she could catch them. I did their health check and prescribed some antibiotic drops for the kittens' gooey eyes.

The pit bull's owner was easy to find in the files by going back to the month before Judith's accident. The shelter took in far fewer dogs than cats.

Tim Gilpin lived on the far side of town. I avoided the road where Judith's accident had taken place, even though it would have been the fastest route, and navigated the more direct route riddled with stop signs and traffic lights instead. The last thing I needed to do before talking to the man who'd potentially sabotaged Judith's brake lines was drive along the road where she almost died. I'd either show up at his house too angry to think straight or too scared to go through with talking to him at all.

A car sat in the driveway when I pulled up. I parked along the curb in front of the house and texted Judith that I'd arrived.

His house didn't have a doorbell, so I knocked as loudly as I could.

"In the garage," a man's voice called.

I followed the walkway back to the driveway. The car door on the garage hung open. Inside, a man sat on the ground next to a motorcycle, wrenches spread out around him. Dark splotches of oil dappled the concrete.

My stomach dipped. A man who fixed his own bike would know about brake lines. That evidence was circumstantial at best, but all I needed was enough circumstantial evidence to decide whether Gilpin might have actually been behind the attacks on Judith, Sebastian, and Buddy.

Today was just drop some names, hint at some things, and see how Gilpin would react. If he sounded guilty, I could take what I did find out to Detective MacIntosh.

The man next to the motorcycle didn't so much as glance in my direction. "How can I help you?"

"Are you Tim Gilpin?" I moved around to the front of his motorcycle. The man was in his forties, balding, and a slight shadow across his cheeks suggested he hadn't shaved today. "I'm from the animal shelter."

He glanced up. His expression stayed flat. "What do you want? You already gave my dogs away to another home. I don't have any more pets for you to steal."

His voice was colder than when he'd first asked how he could help me. He didn't hold my gaze. He swapped the wrench in his hand for a smaller one and went back to work on the bike.

He didn't seem at all nervous about me being here. I was no more significant than the fly also buzzing around him and occasionally trying to settle on the chrome of his motorcycle.

His calm demeanor was actually good. Detecting lying wasn't as easy as shows like *The Mentalist* made it seem. Liars didn't give off a specific tell. If they did, the police wouldn't need polygraphs, and even those weren't accurate enough to be admissible in court. The key was to see if anything you said made a person nervous or uncomfortable. Did they deflect when you asked a question? Or, at least, that's what all my research on *how to tell if someone is lying to you* turned up after Sebastian cheated on me.

I stepped to the right, behind Tim's motorcycle and directly in his line of sight. Well, my shoes were in his line of sight. Time to see if he recognized Judith's name. "Originally, I think you talked to Judith, the shelter manager, about your dogs. Is that right?"

He shrugged. "I talked to a lot of people at the shelter about trying to get my dogs back, but yeah, one of them was named Judith." An impish smile slipped across his lips. "Called her Judy just to tick her off."

He hadn't shown any signs of guilt at the mention of her name. The way he kept working with steady hands and no hesitation made it seem like Judith's name wasn't any more important to him than any of the other shelter employees. Surely if he'd damaged her car, he should have had more of a reaction. Sabotaging a person's car was personal. Would he have found it so amusing to annoy a person he planned to later kill?

I needed to push a little more. "Judith's out after a car accident, and the veterinarian you dealt with, Dr. Clunes, recently passed away so—"

"Look, lady, do you have a reason for being here or not?" He stood up, grabbed a rag, and wiped grease off his hands. "I have to get this bike fixed and back to its owner by tomorrow. You took away my other income when you took my dogs, so the least you can do is stay out of my way now. It's not like chatting with you is going to get me my dogs back."

A band of tension ran through the muscles in my stomach. He was definitely still angry, but it was in an I've-moved-on kind of way. He didn't want to waste his time talking about something he couldn't change. He seemed to want nothing to do with me or anyone else associated with the shelter.

This couldn't be a dead end.

He gathered up the tools from the floor and carried

them over to a neatly arranged pegboard hanging on the wall.

The smell of gasoline and metal clogged my head. I couldn't hang out here forever. Eventually he'd order me to leave. One more try. Besides, I had five more minutes before I needed to text Judith again.

"I'm actually here to talk to you about the threats you and your supporters sent to the shelter. We'd rather not take this to the police."

I planted my hands on my hips and forced confidence into my voice.

"You already reported the threats to the police months ago." He didn't turn around to look at me. His voice was tired and annoyed. "You want to report us a second time even though we've stopped? You don't have enough to do to keep you busy otherwise?"

The threats had stopped, yes, but the actions hadn't. It was a Hail Mary, but Edith seemed convinced that the people wanting to free his pit bull were somehow responsible for Buddy's poisoning. Maybe if I accused him of that, too, the preponderance of things he'd done would crack his calm. "That was before a dog was injured. We need to make sure that your group doesn't hurt any more innocent animals."

Tim turned around, a screwdriver still in his hand. He set it down on a bench. His eyebrows were drawn into a V between his eyes. "What are you talking about?"

Finally. At least that got a reaction. I moved a bit closer to the garage door, just in case. No harm in having an exit strategy. "Someone in the group you organized to protest the seizure of your dogs poisoned a small dog in retaliation. It's our job to protect animals, so I wanted to come talk to you about getting your people under control before we took this to the police."

His lips pulled down at the corners, and he scrubbed a hand along his jeans, leaving a faint smudge behind. "Everyone I recruited to help me protest loves dogs. Yeah, some of them took things too far and threatened the shelter staff, but we wouldn't hurt an animal. We wouldn't have even done anything to the shelter itself. Too many animals who might get hurt. If a dog was hurt, that wasn't us."

The tone of his voice was...insulted. Like how could I ever suspect they would stoop to harming animals? But if they hadn't poisoned Buddy, then perhaps they hadn't damaged Judith's car or killed Sebastian, either.

Still, they had made threats.

Tim didn't look like he was even considering attacking me with any of the wrenches near him, so it should be safe to push him a little more. I had to be sure he was telling the truth. If this was a dead end, then we had even bigger problems than I'd thought.

I licked my lips. "Do you think anyone in your group would have followed through on the threats toward the shelter staff?"

The way he shook his head clearly said *You're nuts*. "Not anyone I asked for help. The threats were just to see if they'd give in under pressure. No one was going to go through with it. Not even me. I loved my dogs, but they weren't worth going to prison over."

Something in the way he said that. I closed my eyes for a second. What was I missing? This was no different from diagnosing an animal who couldn't tell me what was wrong. Tells could be so subtle when an animal was sick. Especially with cats because they lived as both predator and prey, and they had the survival instinct to hide any vulnerability. You had to watch for the tiny things—drinking a little more water, hesitancy to use their litter box, a tiny sneeze, a little scratch, or nothing more than the look in their eyes.

The answer hovered a finger's breadth out of reach as I scrabbled for it.

Not anyone he'd asked for help, he'd said. *His dogs weren't worth going to prison over.*

That was it. For him, this had all been about his dogs. He'd asked people to call the shelter and protest to help him get his dogs back. Once his dogs were sent away and rehomed, it was over for him.

But Pastor Keith had said there was pressure from outside the town to overturn the ban. Not everyone involved cared about Tim's dogs. For some people, the situation might have become about Mayor Edith's dangerous breed ban. Tim had set the ball rolling. Perhaps it'd rolled away from him. "Were people involved in the protesting and threats who weren't part of your group?"

"Yeah." Tim tugged on his earlobe, the first sign of ill

ease since I'd arrived. "Near the end. I was complaining in the bigger online forums. The OABSL—Owners Against Breed-Specific Legislation—must have heard about it there because they reached out to me. All of a sudden, the protests were fifty people instead of five."

The name sounded vaguely familiar. Whoever they were, they made Tim uncomfortable, and he didn't strike me as a man who was easily rattled.

My internal clock said I was close to when I needed to text Judith that I was safe, but I didn't want to risk even a small pause in the conversation. Tim could clam up. "But the OABSL wasn't necessarily working with you?"

"They weren't working with me at all. When they started slashing the tires of the shelter employees, we backed out." Tim grabbed a greasy rag off the bench and rubbed it over his hands again. Whether they were cleaner afterward was questionable. "I just wanted my dogs back. They wanted to get the law changed. They said they'd do whatever it took to make that happen. That was more than I bargained for."

They'd been willing to go further than he had. How much farther? "Do you think they might have resorted to violence?"

A muscle pulsed in Tim's cheek, as if he'd clamped his teeth down. He held up his hands. "I'm not getting drawn back into this. I cut my losses for a reason. You want someone to narc on them, you gotta find someone else."

His whole form looked tense. The OABSL made him more than uncomfortable. Whatever they'd suggested to him, he was afraid of them. Afraid that what they were planning would end up getting him sent to prison.

My stomach turned, and bile burned the back of my throat. I swallowed once, twice. I'd been wrong about Tim. But it sounded like I'd been right that someone was determined to hurt the people who were perceived as supporting the ban. Someone at OABSL might have been behind Judith's accident, Sebastian's death, and Buddy's poisoning. "Did you have a contact person, or do you know who was in charge?"

"I told you. I didn't get tangled up with them." Tim picked up two wrenches and strode back to the motorcycle. "Cash and June's DNA tests came back, the shelter folks knew from their ages that I'd bought them after the ban, breaking the law, and I took the deal for no fines in exchange for not causing any more trouble. That was it for me. I'm out of this town soon as I can sell my house."

My phone pinged. I glanced at the text.

Judith's name was at the top of the message. *You're a minute late! Thirty seconds and I call the police.*

I hurried for the door, typing a reply as I went. "Thanks for your help," I called back to Tim.

He grunted in response.

I abandoned my text and called Judith instead. "I'm fine. Tim Gilpin wasn't involved."

"You're sure?" Judith exhaled the words. Her relief

was probably more because I was okay than that Tim Gilpin was innocent.

I filled her in on everything he'd told me.

Judith sucked in a slow breath. "I didn't realize the OABSL got involved. When it comes to people who are against legislation targeting specific breeds of dogs, they're like the pedophile priest among Christians. They're the outlier who gives others who hold similar beliefs a bad name. Their website uses inflammatory language like *canine genocide*. They're militant. I've even heard they've overturned the cars of government officials who support breed-specific laws."

Which was still a step below physically harming anyone, but not necessarily a far step. Justifying evil tended to be a slippery slope.

And they didn't sound like a group that knew how to stop once they entered a fight. "Has the council set the date for the next meeting?"

Paster Keith had told Edith he planned to revisit the ban at the next council meeting. As soon as the OABSL learned it was on the docket, Judith would be in danger again. They'd still be working under the assumption that she was going to support it.

"Next week." Judith's voice was soft. "Keith called my cell this afternoon, trying to reach you. He thought you'd like to speak at the meeting."

One week. My throat squeezed shut, and I couldn't get air in or words out. Even if I went to Detective MacIntosh right now, and even if he believed me that someone in OABSL was behind everything that had happened, a week wasn't enough time for him to find and arrest whoever was behind the attacks. I'd tell him immediately anyway.

But how was I supposed to keep Judith safe between now and when he could make an arrest?

15

"I'm not coming straight home." I started my car and waited for my phone to connect to Bluetooth so I could continue my conversation with Judith. "I want to swing by the police station first."

Telling Detective MacIntosh everything I'd learned might not protect Judith, but it was the best plan I had at present.

Judith promised to send me a link to the OABSL website so I could show it to Detective MacIntosh, then we disconnected the call.

I signaled and pulled away from Tim Gilpin's house. If I could get ahold of Maeve, I'd have enough time on the drive to fill her in too. She deserved to know.

I told my car to call her phone. She answered on the first ring, and I told her everything I'd told Judith.

"You need to go to Detective MacIntosh immediately." Maeve's tone implied that I wouldn't have thought of that on my own if she hadn't been there to help me decide what to do. "I'll go with you. He might try to brush you off otherwise."

What was I—a three-year-old who needed constant monitoring? The little girl who cried wolf who no one would believe unless someone else vouched for her? How long would it take her to realize I hadn't survived this long without having some brains in my head? "I can go myself. I'm already on my way there."

"You can pick me up on the way. My parents' house isn't far from the station." Her voice was farther away, as if she'd set down the phone to put her shoes on. "I want to go." The volume went back to normal. "I need to go."

The last sentence was rushed, a note of desperation creeping into it.

Judith's words earlier, when we'd been talking about why she hadn't ratted me out about keeping Tanglefoot in the shed, flooded back into my mind. I'd asked her not to. I'd needed her not to. That was all that mattered. Maeve's words weren't exactly a request, but needing something—even when other people couldn't understand why you needed it—well, I'd been there.

And I *had* wanted to be more like Judith.

"Give me the address."

Maeve waited at the end of the driveway when I pulled up. She wore a flower-patterned sundress and strappy sandals. I glanced at my rumpled t-shirt and jean shorts. Okay, so maybe having her along wouldn't hurt in the credibility department.

The same woman was behind the desk at the police station as when we'd come last time. We stepped up to the plexiglass shield.

"Here to see Detective MacIntosh again?" Her gaze swept over Maeve and then me, and her eyebrows rose slightly. "You ladies are sure here a lot lately. I hope this is actually important."

One of her eyebrows lifted a touch higher than the other. Almost as if she were implying we were hanging around Detective MacIntosh for reasons other than the case. Had that happened a lot since he'd moved to Arbor? Women trumping up reasons to speak with him? He wasn't *that* good-looking.

If that were the case, at least she'd think it was Maeve, not me, who had her eyes on Detective MacIntosh. Between the two of us, I clearly had wingwoman written all over me.

I glanced at Maeve, but she wasn't looking at me, prepared to share an amused smile. She was blinking too fast, and she looked like she'd swallowed her tongue.

Crap. She was trying not to cry.

I tapped a finger on the plexiglass, and the woman turned her stare my way. "I'd say that the murder investigation of her fiancé is important." I added extra emphasis to *fiancé*. "So if you could let Detective MacIntosh know that Maeve Stokes and Zoe Stephenson are here to see him…"

Two blotches of color stained the woman's cheeks, and she dialed the numbers into the phone.

We settled in on the chairs to wait, Maeve gracefully tucking her skirt underneath her as she sat.

Five minutes later, the woman rapped on the plexiglass. "Detective MacIntosh says to send you through. His office is the one to the left."

Apparently, this time he wasn't willing to speak to us in the reception area. A way of making sure we knew who was in charge?

We went through the door the woman pointed at and down a hallway. The interview room I'd been placed in and a few other doors opened off the hallway, but all the doors were closed.

The hallway opened into a much larger room than the reception area, with desks laid out in a grid. Detectives in suits and officers in uniforms were scattered around the room, a few talking in clusters but most working at one of the desks. The faint smells of stale coffee and chili hung in the air.

An officer with a Tupperware container in one hand and a spoon in the other stopped next to us. Steam rose from the container. "You here to see someone?"

"Detective MacIntosh," Maeve said. Her voice was clear and sharp again.

The officer led the way as if he didn't want us wandering off. The back of the room had two offices fronted by large glass windows. The plaque on the right door read *Chief of Police*. The plaque on the left read *Chief of Detectives*.

So Detective MacIntosh wasn't a simple detective. Good thing I hadn't known that to begin with or I would have been even more nervous when he seemed to want to lay Sebastian's murder at my feet. Though it did beg the question of why the Chief of Detectives would be the one to help the animal shelter with by-law infractions the way Judith said.

He couldn't possibly be an animal lover, could he? He didn't exactly come across as the cuddle-on-the-couch-with-furry-creatures type. Maybe he was interested in Judith. I shuddered. Detective MacIntosh glaring at me over the turkey every Thanksgiving and Christmas was not my idea of a restful holiday.

Maeve knocked.

"Come in," Detective MacIntosh's voice called.

We entered, and he looked up from his computer.

One side of his lips twisted up. "Do you two go everywhere together now?" He motioned toward the chairs in front of his desk. "They're more comfortable than the ones in the reception area. I figured that if you're going to keep showing up, you could come to me this time."

I placed my hands on my hips. "Would you rather we didn't bring you important information about a murder case?"

He looked at me, deadpan. "We might differ on what's important, but I didn't send you away, did I?"

Maeve sat, crossed her legs, and made a hurry-up motion with her hand. "Can you two continue whatever this is later?"

I huffed. It's not like we were flirting. But she did have a point. Neither of us wanted to spend more time with Detective MacIntosh than we had to. "I think I might know who killed Sebastian. They might also have cut my sister's brakes and poisoned the mayor's dog."

Detective MacIntosh straightened in his chair. "Go on."

I explained what Tim Gilpin told me and what Judith said about OABSL. I pulled up their website on my phone and went around his desk. I held it so he could see the screen and scrolled through some of their pages.

He leaned in, his head near mine. He smelled good, like trees and fresh air, rather than the overpowering synthetic scents of aftershave and body spray that some men doused themselves in.

I jerked upright. What was wrong with me? Thinking about how he smelled! The receptionist's needling and Maeve's offhand comment were putting thoughts in my head.

I backed away until I was standing beside Maeve on the opposite side of the desk again.

He leaned back in his chair. "That's a lot of guesswork, but I'll send someone to speak to the head of this group. We've hit a dead end on the financial paperwork you gave us. Nothing unusual turned up in Dr. Clunes' bank account or on his credit cards to suggest he had a gambling problem or an illegal source of income. We'll keep looking."

Maeve pressed a hand over her lips. She slowly lowered her hand. "It's good to hear not everything I thought I knew about him was wrong."

Good for her, but bad for the case. And Sebastian had still been hiding something about the financial discrepancies.

"Is there anything else?" Detective MacIntosh tapped a pen on his desk. "Or can I get back to work?"

I scowled at him. "That's all for now. I'll—"

Maeve linked her arm with mine. "Thank you, Detective. That's all." She ushered me from the room. "You don't know how to walk away while you're ahead, do you?" Her words were hissed almost under her breath. "Antagonizing him will only make him less likely to listen if you do find out something else important in the future."

Why did she have to have a point? "Hopefully there won't be anything more in the future. And hopefully he finds who did this soon. I'm worried about Judith, what with the council meeting coming up."

Not that Maeve needed to know I was worried. But we were kind of allies in all this now.

Maeve released my arm in a way that said she was finally sure I wasn't going to stalk back to Detective MacIntosh's office so I could have the last word. "Not to mention your safety as well. After all, it's Sebastian who ended up dead, not Judith."

My safety? I'd only be in danger if the OABSL thought I was going to support the dangerous breed ban. Which I wasn't. But they might think I was. An ache bloomed behind my eyes. Perfect. One more thing to worry about.

And they'd perfected their methods now. Their attempt on Judith's life failed, so they'd made sure their attack on Sebastian couldn't. If they wanted to kill me, they'd take the same precautions.

"That almost sounds like you're worried about me." I'd meant my words to sound flippant. They came out sounding faint instead.

"I'm worried about all of us. I think we need to make it public."

I waited to answer until we were past the snooty woman in the reception area and back out onto the street. "Make what public?"

Maeve rolled her eyes. "Our opposition to the ban, of course. If we all, veterinary staff and shelter staff, make it clear that we want to see the ban repealed, then OABSL will have no reason to target any of us."

If she'd been a man, I would have kissed her. The solution was so simple I should have thought about it before. "Edith Cameron won't be safe. Neither will Buddy." Neither would any of the council members who voted in favor of keeping the ban in place.

"No." Maeve pursed her lips. "Not in the short-term.

But if we succeed in convincing the council to overturn the ban, the OABSL people will leave Arbor alone for good."

A smile crept onto my lips. Maybe we really could do this. "Not to mention they'll be lulled into a false sense of security. People who feel safe make mistakes, and mistakes will help Detective MacIntosh finally catch Sebastian's killer."

16

An hour later, Kat, Maeve, and I were at my kitchen table for what Maeve called a "strategy session" to put together a plan to convince the town councilors to overturn the dangerous breed ban. Judith was in the bedroom, on the phone with Bob Bremnes at the animal shelter.

Maeve crossed her legs but kept her back perfect-posture straight. "I should be the one to speak with the councilors, don't you think? You and Kat can handle stuffing the fliers into mailboxes and encouraging people to talk to their representatives."

Her words sounded as if there was a slight hidden in them even though her tone didn't carry one. Why should she be the one to speak to the councilors instead of me? "I'm the veterinarian. My opinion will carry more weight."

Maeve's gaze slid over me quickly, as if she were

going to make a comment about my appearance and how I didn't dress like someone people would take seriously. "I know the people on the town council."

I crossed my arms over my chest. "You know who they are. I probably know them personally. I grew up here."

Not that knowing them would always work in my favor. Not with the *blood will tell* crowd who condemned me for Tonya's crimes. But some people would listen to me because they respected my parents.

Kat's head twisted back and forth, her gaze bouncing between us. She opened her mouth as if to say something, then shook her head, and closed it again. She probably thought getting between us was about as wise as trying to separate two fighting cats with your bare hands.

Maeve picked a piece of something too small for me to see off her skirt. "You can be a bit…passionate at times."

My chest felt like something was spinning inside it, waiting to break loose. Holding things inside wasn't necessarily a better way to be. People who did that ended up with ulcers and high blood pressure. "Maybe passion's what we need right now. Edith certainly isn't going to submissively roll over and show her belly. She'll be advocating for her side with everything she has. If I can win her over, the rest of the council will likely fall into line."

Kat's feet bobbed on the floor as if sitting still this

long was more than she could tolerate. "There are twelve people on the council and only one week. So maybe you two could each take six?" Her voice lifted on the end as if she wasn't sure what kind of reception to expect from her suggestion. "I'm happy to coordinate whatever other volunteers we get from the shelter staff to do the flyers and other stuff."

"I think that's fair," Maeve said. "Don't you?"

My mom would have called it hedging our bets. If I came on too strongly with my half of the list, Maeve might win the others over.

Kat's suggestion did make more sense than me trying to speak to more than two councilors a day, plus the mayor. "Alright. We divide and conquer. But I'd like to be the one to speak to the mayor. She might still be grateful enough about me helping Buddy to listen to me."

Maeve grabbed a piece of paper and jotted down names. She had the list of town councilors memorized? Who *did* that?

She slid the paper across the table. "I gave you the mayor and the councilors who come from your side of town. That makes the most sense."

The council meeting was next Friday night. I already knew Pastor Keith was in favor of repealing the ban, so that left me with five councilors and Edith Cameron. I knew just where I wanted to start. When Edith came to the vet clinic to visit Buddy on her Monday lunch break, I'd be ready.

***

Edith opened the kennel door, and Buddy practically launched himself into her arms.

I stood to the side, giving them a moment.

His little tongue flashed out, licking every inch of her exposed skin, her shirt, and the scarf draped around her neck. In all her regular lunchtime visits since Buddy had come to the clinic, she hadn't once complained about his enthusiasm messing up her makeup or leaving dog hair on her clothes, though she did pull a lint roller from her purse as soon as he went back into his kennel.

Her problem with what she considered dangerous breeds didn't seem to be a problem with dogs in general. Her problem didn't even seem to be with large breed dogs. A Great Dane had been heading out when she came into the clinic, and she asked permission to pet him.

Buddy wriggled in her arms so energetically I wasn't sure how she managed to hold onto him. The first day she'd come to visit, I'd said she could take him home with her, and she'd pointed out that we had enough kennel space to keep him until he'd fully recovered.

Part of my plan included leveraging the gratitude she hopefully felt toward me for saving her dog to at least get her to listen to me. I needed to tread carefully, but really, Buddy had been fully recovered for days.

"He's been eating well," I said. "And his energy levels

are great. Would you like to set up a time to take him home?"

She tucked him under her arm like a football, and he settled slightly. "Almost. You wouldn't rush a surgery patient through recovery, and I don't want Buddy rushed, either. You should know that by now."

He no longer needed medical care, so all we were really doing at this point was boarding him. Even Maeve hadn't been able to convince her of that, though. "Animals often recover better in a familiar environment."

She shook her head. "No. I don't think so. If I brought him home now, I'd simply need to bring him back in every day or have you make a house call to check on his progress. I won't risk it."

Arguing with her wasn't going to win me any points on either front. "We can keep him for another couple of days to be sure, and I'll check him myself every day."

She gave me a look that said obviously I would. Wasn't that my job, after all?

I held out my arms for Buddy, but she placed him back into the kennel herself. He curled up onto the blanket with a huff and a resigned sigh. Unlike many of the animals we got in, he'd clearly been crate-trained well.

Edith turned to go. I couldn't delay any longer. Judith and I had once again written up a script and practiced it the night before—something I wouldn't have embarrassed myself with by telling Maeve when she suggested I'd get carried away in my conversations. But it did help. Judith let me know when things I planned to say might come across as confrontational or pushy or judgmental.

Now all I needed to do was stick to the script better than I had when I came asking Maeve for a job.

"I did have one more thing I wanted to talk to you about."

She had her hand in her purse, and it came out with her phone. She glanced at the screen. "Make it quick. I have another appointment in fifteen minutes."

No pressure. "I wanted to talk to you about a paper I read published by the Toronto Humane Society in Canada. Ontario has a pit bull ban similar to our town's ban. They found that even though their numbers of pit bulls have gone down, their number of dog bites have actually gone up. Their conclusion was that serious dog bites are more a result of negligent or unskilled owners than they are about any specific breed of dog."

My words came out stilted. Edith would likely be able to tell that I'd written the words out ahead of time and memorized them. Hopefully that wouldn't matter. Hopefully she'd only take me more seriously because of it. Preparing and memorizing meant I took this seriously enough not to just yell at her that *There are no bad dogs, only bad owners*, which had been my instinct until Judith chimed in.

I did not want to prove Maeve right that I was "too passionate."

Edith dropped her phone back in her purse with

more force than was necessary. She turned to face me. "That's Canada."

Because the dogs in Canada were more vicious than the dogs here? "It's not just Canada. There are similar results from Ireland, and from here in the U.S., too. Iowa."

I felt like I'd read studies from other states as well, but I hadn't expected her to question the study itself.

Edith put a hand on her scarf. "I could cite as many statistics to show that breed-specific bans have helped. When the council originally discussed this, I even printed off copies of a 2011 study for them showing that pit bull bites are more severe than those by other dogs."

My throat tightened with all the things I wanted to say. I wanted to question the methods of her study even though I'd never read it. It felt like she was questioning my competency as a veterinarian.

Which was silly. She'd just insisted that I keep Buddy with us a few more days because she was convinced he needed me to check him every day in case he relapsed—which wasn't even possible for a poisoning case.

Our disagreement wasn't about me and whether I could do my job. It wasn't even about me and whether I knew more about animals in general than she did. This wasn't about me at all, despite how her questioning me made me feel.

Not all vets agreed on the dangerous nature or non-dangerous nature of certain breeds. In some countries,

Great Danes, like the one she passed on the way in, were banned merely because of their size.

I couldn't lose my temper right now. Zoe the Volcano needed to stay dormant.

I imagined a glacier toppling over into a volcano and hardening the lava into rock. I could be firm and strong without burning everyone around me. I could.

I drew in an additional calming breath. "I've treated a lot of animals, and my experience has been that what would help more is a mandatory training program for all dog owners. That would reduce the number of dog bites overall, and it wouldn't penalize certain breeds for stereotypes that might or might not be true."

Edith's hand pressed flat against the base of her neck. Her face had paled, making her lipstick and blush look stark and almost gaudy against her skin. "That's a good idea, but as an additional item to make our town even safer. Not as a replacement for the ban."

The haughty tone in her voice suggested that I didn't understand and never would. As if I were too naive and optimistic. Or too driven by my own agenda.

I didn't have an agenda. I didn't own one of the breeds on the list.

I clenched my jaw. "I'm not talking about—"

Edith raised her free hand, the one that wasn't practically clenched around her neck, in a *stop* gesture. A muscle jumped in her jaw. She pulled her scarf down. The skin on her neck was puckered and red.

"Do you think anything you say will convince me to

change my mind?" Her voice was low, hissing out between her teeth.

Buddy let out a keening whine in his kennel, but she didn't look at him.

"Reconstructive surgeries couldn't get rid of all the scars, and I still have nightmares. Not to mention the way I have to wear turtlenecks or scarfs even in weather that would make someone who grew up in the Sahara Desert sweat because otherwise this"—she pointed at the damaged skin—"is all people see."

My hand went to my own neck before I could stop it, and my stomach rolled over. Stories of attack survivors were all over the Internet, but to see the aftereffects in person was like the difference between seeing a house fire on TV compared to standing in the street and watching your neighbor's house burn, the heat slicking your skin and ash pluming in the air. The difference between *That's sad* and *That could have been me.*

"I'm sorry that happened to you." Hopefully she would hear in my tone that I meant it. It was a miracle she wasn't afraid of all dogs. With a neck bite severe enough to leave scars like hers, it was a miracle she'd survived. No child deserved the pain and fear she must have experienced. "Any bitten child is one too many, but there are more effective ways to keep everyone safe than to ban certain breeds."

She let her scarf slide back into place. "What's more important? Protecting children or allowing people the freedom to own whatever breed of dog they want?"

I could see her speaking at the town council meeting, arguing that very point. Making anyone who disagreed with her seem like a selfish monster. Who would try to argue that children's safety wasn't more important? "That's a false dichotomy. Pit bull-type dogs, properly raised, make loving family pets."

"All the mandates in the world won't make sure they're all *properly raised*." The derision in her tone, the fury in her gaze—in her eyes, I was no better than someone in prison for child endangerment. "Before I became mayor, my daughter was almost bitten by a pit bull that got away from its owner. I will not put my daughter or any child in this town at risk of going through what I went through. If people want to own one of the breeds on our list, they can go somewhere else. We don't say no one can own them. We only say they can't own them here. As long as I'm mayor of this town, I will do whatever it takes to keep it safe."

17

I closed the vet clinic door behind the emergency case that had arrived five minutes before we were supposed to close. The cat's respiratory infection would clear up nicely with the antibiotics I'd prescribed, but she'd already been refusing to eat because of the congestion in her nose. Had her owner waited to bring her in until we opened again on Monday, things could have been dire. Cats weren't like humans or dogs who could survive for a week or two without food as long as they had water. A cat's organs could shut down within three days without protein. I'd had to stay and treat her.

I glanced at the clock: 6:55 pm. Good thing Maeve and Kat had gone ahead without me to the council meeting. Five minutes wasn't enough time to make it across town even if I sped. And, according to Pastor Keith, the ban was first on the agenda for the evening because it was considered old business.

I locked the clinic door and jogged to my car. One side of town to the other, through town, with stoplights.

If I went through town, I risked arriving too late to speak.

And the vote was going to be close. I tallied them again in my head. Of the six councilors I'd talked to, Pastor Keith and two others had said they planned to vote in favor of abolishing the ban. The other three told me they planned to vote in favor of keeping it. The councilors Maeve spoke to were three voting to keep the ban, two to abolish, and one undecided.

In the case of a 6-6 council decision, the mayor had the tiebreaker vote. Edith would never break the tie in our favor. Our best hope was to sway the one undecided councilor at the meeting tonight. All the statistics and studies we'd found and printed off were in my car.

I started my car. I could *not* be late.

But the quicker route to town hall involved taking the road where Judith had her accident.

My stomach seized like I'd swallowed rocks.

"Stop being a coward," I said out loud. "No one's going to mess with your car. The OABSL should be rolling out the red carpet for you."

Besides, I couldn't avoid that road forever. And my car had looked exactly the way I'd left it that morning. Not like that meant anything. Judith's car had probably looked completely normal, too.

Just a quick check, for safety's sake, and then I'd buck up and take the river road. I climbed out of my car, turned on the flashlight on my phone, and knelt on the cement of the parking lot. Stones poked into my knees. I shined the light on the ground and up under the chassis of my car. No fluid leaks.

Thunder boomed in the distance. I scrambled to my feet and climbed back into my car. Better to move quickly for two reasons now—if it started to pour, I definitely didn't want to be taking the tight turns on the river road. Especially if the wind kicked up. The conditions were ripe for a tornado. Arbor had never been hit directly, but we still had enough damage from high wind speeds whenever one passed nearby.

Rain spattered down on my windshield, and I flicked my wipers on to high speed, the soothing *whisk-whisk* noises filling my car.

I rolled up to the stop sign before the turn onto the river road and hit my brakes hard. My car jerked to a stop, slamming me against my seatbelt. No harm checking them just in case. I'd creep down the hill when I reached it, riding my brakes the whole way.

I turned onto the river road. A gust of wind hit my car, rocking it. Tension twined around my head and pressed on my temples. My chest weighed twice what the rest of me did.

You had to be afraid before you could be brave. No road was going to defeat me.

The rain pounded harder on my windshield. Of course, now I could add the fear of hydroplaning. I slowed.

The road dropped from sight, marking the start of the hill. I eased my foot off on the gas and over onto the brake. Who cared if I wore my brakes out quicker this way? It was worth it.

I hit the lip of the hill and headed down.

My car sputtered and jerked. My heart beat high and hard, as if it were trying to climb out of my body and escape. I slammed on the brakes, and my car lurched to a stop. My seatbelt locked into place. I leaned my head back. My brakes still worked. Whatever this was had to be a glitch.

I lifted my foot off the brake. My car eased forward again, drawn by the momentum of gravity.

The car reached the bottom of the hill, and my lungs opened up. I sucked in a huge breath. There. See? No problem.

I touched my foot to the accelerator, and my car jerked again. A sputtering noise barely loud enough to be heard over the rain reached me. I eased to the side of the road. My car rolled to a stop.

And died.

Had I killed it somehow by riding the brakes? Burned something out? I knew basic maintenance for putting air in my tires or swapping out windshield wipers, but I couldn't tell what the weird noises meant.

This couldn't be happening.

The clock on my dash read 7:05 pm. The town council meeting would have started by now.

I dialed Maeve's cell number. The call went directly

to voicemail. She must have already turned off her phone for the council meeting. That would be Maeve-like, turning it off in advance.

I called Kat. Hers went straight to voicemail as well. Obviously it would. She'd be sitting with Maeve, and there's no way Maeve would have left that up to Kat to remember. She'd probably ordered Kat to take out her phone and turn it off at the same time as she did her own.

Walking it was. At least I was wearing comfortable shoes.

I stepped out into the rain. The cold hit me like I'd leaped into the lake for a Polar Bear Run, and the wind tore at my clothes. On the bright side, I wouldn't be sweaty when I got there. I bowed my head into the wind and trudged forward.

A streak of lightning lit the sky, and I jumped.

A wiser version of me probably would have given up on the town council meeting and huddled in her car waiting for a tow truck. But I was not giving up when we were so close. Hopefully there were enough tall trees out here that I wouldn't become a crispy-fried Zoe from the lightning.

My shoes squished with every step I took, and shivers raced over my skin.

What could have happened to my car? Even when money was tight, I maintained my vehicle. My dad always said that was an area where you shouldn't skimp because you didn't want to end up stranded on the side of the road.

Yet here I was, stranded on the side of the road anyway.

Something must have gone wrong with my car. This didn't seem like sabotage. My brakes worked. My car had just given up and stopped. No one was even around to run me down while I walked. No one had sneaked up on my car to try to drag me off into the woods. I was cold and my nose was running, but otherwise, I was unharmed. And I couldn't have made it clearer that I was *against* the breed ban if I'd stood on the steps of town hall with a bullhorn and shouted it. OABSL didn't have any reason to try to stop me.

The glow of the supermarket cut through the rain and gloom. How long had I been walking? My feet ached, suggesting I'd been traveling for a while. I didn't dare bring my phone out into this downpour to check.

I'd have missed the old business at the meeting for sure. If I was lucky, they'd let me speak anyway. Surely there was some leeway to reopen a motion before the meeting closed.

Buildings rose up around me. Not much farther now.

The sidewalk started, and I passed the drug store and the dental office. Town Hall stood a block ahead, its tall, peaked roof distinct from the other buildings around it.

The parking lot was much too empty. According to

Judith, the council meetings were normally full. I broke into a jog.

I ran up the steps and burst through the doors.

The room was only a third full, most people standing around in small groups, chatting. The table at the front where the mayor and councilors sat was empty.

I yanked my phone out. Eight thirty-five. It'd taken me ninety minutes to walk here thanks to the wind and rain.

"Where have you been?" Maeve broke away from the cluster of people she'd been standing with off to one side and stalked toward me. Her gaze slid over me, and her eyebrows rose up almost to her hair line. "And what happened to you?"

I pulled my scrubs top away from where it'd plastered to my body. As soon as I let go, it went back, as if my skin and my wet shirt carried opposite charges. I didn't have a good enough figure for a skin-tight outfit, but apparently, I didn't have a choice. At least my shirt wasn't white. "My c-car broke d-down on the river road."

My teeth chattered so hard that my words came out with a stutter. How was it possible that I felt colder now than I had when I was walking? It had to be all the adrenaline draining from my body and the fact that I was standing still.

Maeve's eyebrows rose—impossibly—higher. "You walked all the way here?"

"Everyone had their p-phones off for the m-meeting." I wrapped my arms around myself. "D-did we win?"

Maeve shook her head.

I stumbled back a step. My legs went limp, and all I wanted to do was sit down. Deep down I'd been so sure we were going to be able to change things. How had we failed?

"Zoe!"

Pastor Keith jogged from the same direction as Maeve had. His gaze swept over me, and before I knew what was happening, he wrapped a light jacket around my shoulders.

He quickly ran his hands up and down my arms, eyes holding my gaze. "We were worried about you."

The warmth spread up into my cheeks, which thankfully probably only brought them back to their original color with how cold I was. Not the right time to be distracted.

I tore my gaze away from Pastor Keith's and forced it onto Maeve. "By how much?"

Pastor Keith stopped rubbing my arms. A little shiver ran over me at the loss of the warmth.

Maeve glanced in his direction. "Eight to four against."

Eight to four. Not even a tie. Not just the undecided vote deciding to support keeping the ban. We'd lost one of the votes we were sure of. "Did you speak?"

Maeve nodded. "So did Kat, but we didn't have all the statistics and studies you found. We only had our personal opinions and experience. It wasn't enough. Other people stood up and talked about why they'd feel safer if the ban stayed in place."

I wiped wet hair off my forehead. I'd warmed up to the point that I felt clammy. Clammy and deep-bone weary, like I could sleep as long as Sleeping Beauty and still wake up exhausted. Everything we'd done this week—all the phone calls and fliers, all the councilors we'd spoken to—had been for nothing.

Well, not entirely for nothing. I'd spent hours wheeling Judith around town, stuffing flyers and talking to people. At least OABSL shouldn't try to hurt her again.

Though all the people who'd voted in favor of keeping the ban in place were now in danger. "Who switched?"

Something shifted in Pastor Keith's posture, as if he went from standing at ease to standing at attention. There was a sudden stiffness to his body language. "I voted to keep the ban in place."

His jacket constricted my movement and hung too heavy on my shoulders. I shrugged it off and held it between my fingertips.

When we'd talked, he'd been on my side, hadn't he? He'd *sounded* like he was on my side. He must have been. During the confrontation with Edith the first time I met her, he'd been the one to mention revisiting the breed ban because she was getting power-mad. I hadn't imagined those things.

Unless he'd lied, saying one thing to my face and intending to do another all along. Why would he do that?

It was the question I'd asked myself for months after Sebastian cheated on me. This wasn't nearly as extreme, but I'd started to see Keith as a friend. And he was a pastor. Of all people, I should have been able to trust a pastor.

That tight, painful weight was back in my chest. The common denominator here was me. Was it something I was doing wrong that people I trusted kept lying to me?

I shoved his jacket back toward him. "You could have told me rather than doing it behind my back."

"This wasn't an easy decision." His voice was soft and sad, like he was the one who'd been hurt, not me. "If it'd only been about me, I would have voted against it. But it isn't just about me. I'm a representative, and the people in the community that I represent wanted me to vote to keep the ban in place."

Tears burned my eyes. I blinked hard. Maeve, Kat, and I had encouraged people to do that very thing with our flyers—speak to your member of the council, we'd told them.

Judith would tell me he'd done the right thing. Elected officials were supposed to abide by the wishes of their constituents.

But I couldn't have done it. I couldn't have voted against my conscience regardless of what the majority of people wanted me to do. Keith shouldn't have, either.

"So you voted to keep in place something that's wrong?"

Maeve glanced behind her and made a little motion with her hands, as if she wanted to remind me that we were still in public. I looked over. The few people left in the room were lingering at the door, as if waiting to see the outcome of this. Let them look. If people wanted to judge me for standing up for what I believed in, so be it.

The muscles around Keith's jaw tightened. "I don't agree with the ban, but it's not morally wrong. No one's trying to make a law to round up all the pit bulls and shoot them."

How could he not get this? It wasn't even that he'd voted against me. Not entirely, anyway. It was that he hadn't told me. "How hard would it have been to give me a call and explain that before you cast your vote?"

"I wanted to weigh all the information presented tonight before I could make a final decision about which way to vote." He shrugged and shook his head. "Knowing my vote wouldn't have changed anything."

I scowled. Stupid reasonable reasons. Even with his vote, we'd have been seven to five, which meant the undecided vote wanted to keep the ban in place, too, but I'd thought Keith had my back. Could something be right and reasonable and still feel like a betrayal?

He lifted a hand in farewell. "See you around." He strode past me.

I spun around to stop him, to find some way to bridge the gap, but he was already out the door.

This day just kept getting better and better.

Maeve looped her umbrella over her wrist. "I'm assuming you need a ride home? It would have been more convenient for Keith to drive you since he lives next door but..."

Her tone made it clear that I'd created a hassle for her, making her go out of her way and probably soaking her seats. I glanced down. Water had dripped into a puddle on the floor around me. *Definitely* soaking her seats.

My chest tightened. Her tone reminded me of when I'd first moved in with my dad, and I'd overheard two women from the church call me a burden. At the time, I had a tendency to steal food. Sometimes to hide in case there wasn't any the next day and sometimes to eat, even if I wasn't hungry, in case it was a while before I'd get to eat again. That had been how I survived with Tonya.

One of the church ladies caught me eating the bread the church had purchased for communion. *Such a shame for Pastor to be burdened with this,* she'd said to the other woman. *She'll cause him nothing but trouble.*

I'd tried to refuse to go to church after that. Church people were mean, I'd told my parents. Weren't church people supposed to be nicer than everyone else?

My mom tried to explain that many people at church were there because they knew they did things they shouldn't, and they wanted to be better—more like Jesus. Sometimes the people there actually seemed worse than other people because the ones with the greatest need for change were the ones who saw their need and came to church.

The concepts went over my head then. All I knew was the doubt that sat in my chest after that. Was I causing problems for my dad? Would he be better off without me? Every time I thought about those women catching me, I felt small and ashamed.

Maeve's comment brought that rushing back. I shouldn't even still remember all that, let alone allow it to bother me. But it was like having a cavity you didn't remember until you took a drink of ice water.

My bad choices were inconveniencing people again.

I wrapped my arms around my middle. "I'll walk."

Maeve pulled her chin back as if I'd tried to spit at her. "Don't be like that. It's still raining out."

I pulled out my phone. I'd call a tow for my car, and then I'd go. My phone refused to turn on. A bead of water dripped down the screen.

I shoved it back into my pocket. "I can't get any wetter."

My throat was too tight, like each thing that had gone wrong had pushed everything up until there wasn't enough space in my body unless I cried and let some of it out. I spun on my heel and sprinted for the door.

Let the few remaining people think whatever they wanted to.

The air outside set the hair on my arms to standing up. The rain had diminished to a drizzle.

Being outside, despite the rain, was almost better. At

least I didn't feel musty and sticky anymore the way I had when my clothes were drying. Tears forced their way out and joined the rain running down my cheeks.

The walk would do me good, even though it probably meant another hour and a half on my feet or more.

I didn't want to go home and tell Judith what had happened or how I'd lashed out at Keith afterward. All my plans had failed, and then I'd insulted the man who saved her. Then I'd made everything worse by snapping at someone who wasn't just my boss but who'd gone out of her way to help me this past week.

So in the span of a night, I'd managed to alienate two people who'd tried to be nice to me. Good thing Kat hadn't still been there or I'd likely have found a way to insult her, too.

This was why I should stick with animals and avoid people.

I wanted to throw my arms around Orion, but I couldn't go home until I felt less like a screwup. Judith didn't need to try to pull me out of a pity party on top of everything else. I needed to regroup and figure out my next step.

Sebastian's killer was still on the loose. We'd probably managed to anger their attacker even more by revisiting and then upholding the ban. Was there anything we could do to help figure out who'd killed him? Anything we hadn't already tried?

The chill was slowing my brain, making all my thoughts move sluggishly across my mind.

A car rolled up beside me. The window on the front passenger's side slid down.

"Stop being stubborn and get in," Maeve's voice yelled from the interior. "I will not have it on my conscience if you get pneumonia."

She'd come after me. I'd metaphorically shoved her away, and she'd gotten in her car and followed me.

The rain had cooled my anger to a sizzle. It hadn't really been directed at her in the first place. I stopped walking, and the car stopped moving.

I slid inside. Maeve had somehow managed to swath her passenger's seat with a split open garbage bag and towels, like she kept some in her trunk in case she needed to pick up a bedraggled hitchhiker. My car had a cat carrier and blankets in the back in case I came across a stray animal I needed to transport. Maybe Detective MacIntosh was more right than he realized. Sebastian did have a type. Our personalities weren't the same, but some of our underlying traits were.

"I think you meant hypothermia, not pneumonia," I said around teeth that had begun to chatter again.

"I most certainly did not." Maeve put the car back into drive. "It's too warm for hypothermia, but if you compromise your immune system by walking around in the rain, you'll be more susceptible to infections and viruses."

She didn't say anything about my outburst. Thankfully. Talk about awkward if she had.

"We don't have to give up if we don't want to." Maeve

pointed a finger toward her glove compartment. "There are napkins in there if you'd like to wipe your face."

By which she probably actually meant *wipe your nose.*

Did she not miss anything? It must be hard for any human to be this put together all the time. I tried, and I didn't come anywhere close.

I took out a napkin and used it. A person could take stubbornness too far, after all.

Both Keith and Edith had said people were afraid. I'd ignored that because it didn't fit with what *I* wanted and what *I* needed. I'd thought I knew better what needed to be done. "Maybe we shouldn't push it anymore. Keith was right. This isn't a moral issue. If people in town want the ban, then it's not up to me to force them to get rid of it."

Maeve made a huffing noise. "The vote was close. Well...close-ish anyway."

That only reminded me of Keith. I couldn't help feeling like I'd broken something there that couldn't be put back together. But that might just be me projecting onto him how I'd feel. Now that I was in Maeve's car, with a little distance from what had happened, it was obvious that he hadn't sold out or intentionally deceived me.

I shifted around. My wet clothes stuck to me in all the wrong places. Sitting here was like being wrapped up in a nest of wet tissues.

Something had been niggling at me since my argument with Keith. The concept of motivations. I'd been motivated in all of this by keeping Judith safe and flushing out Sebastian's killer. "Were our motives right, though? I wanted the ban overturned because I don't believe pit bulls are more dangerous than other dogs, but that wasn't my primary motive for fighting the law now. Was it yours?"

Maeve pressed her lips together in a way that made her mouth look too long. "No. You know it wasn't."

"All I'm saying is that maybe we should let it be until it is."

She made an *mmm* noise, which was probably all the admission of wrong that I'd get out of her. "What do we do now?"

She could only mean one thing—Sebastian's murder. Since when was there a *we*? Yeah, she'd helped me take the paperwork to Detective MacIntosh, and we'd gone together to talk to him about the OABSL lead. And obviously she'd helped me with the plan to keep Judith safe by publicly opposing the ban.

Hmm. Putting that all together *did* sort of amount to a *we*. Like maybe we were moving from *two women Sebastian Clunes proposed to* into *friends*. "For now, we hope whoever hurt Sebastian and Judith doesn't come for the council members who voted to keep the ban in place."

Keith's hurt expression flashed across my mind again, but I shoved it away. My temper had broken a lot of things over the years. I shouldn't be surprised that it'd finally broken a burgeoning friendship. Maybe he would forgive me if I brought more cookies? He'd liked the last ones. Or a whole meal?

If I left this breech unresolved and something happened to him, that'd be hard to live with.

We'd reached the turn that would take us toward my neighborhood.

Maeve hit her signal. "The council members or the mayor. The mayor's probably the one who's most in jeopardy from OABSL."

I sucked in a breath. The last time they hadn't attacked the mayor directly. They'd gone for her dog. I'd thought Edith was jumping to conclusions when she said Buddy's poisoning was all their fault, but in hindsight, the twisted logic made sense. Edith had created a situation where a man had his dog taken away from him. Someone might think it was justice to take her dog away from her in return.

My stomach filled with concrete. "I think we should swing by the clinic before you take me home."

18

Maeve pulled into the clinic's empty parking lot. "There. Can we call this goose chase finished? There's no one here."

"There aren't any cars here, but that doesn't mean there aren't any people here. If someone wanted to hurt Buddy, they'd be smart to park somewhere else and walk. A car at the vet clinic at this time of night would draw attention, even if people only thought that an emergency had come in. Small town gossip would wonder who it was, and any attention is bad attention for someone with criminal intent."

Maeve arched an eyebrow. "They hid their car and walked here in the rain." She ran her gaze over my soaked, bedraggled attire.

The rain made it unlikely that someone had walked here, but they could have been dropped off, or they could have parked one street over. The rain had dropped to a drizzle. With an umbrella, one street was nothing.

I wouldn't be able to stop worrying about it if we left right away. "Let's sit for a minute. At least that way, if anyone comes intending something, they'll keep going."

"Fine." Maeve turned the car off. "But I'm not wasting gas."

I opened my mouth to argue with her but snapped it back shut. As I started to dry, I'd also begun to smell faintly of wet dog. Turning off the car would confine us with that smell and no air circulation. If I told her that, though, she'd refuse to budge. I'd let her experience the smell for herself. The car would be back on in around a minute.

A quick flash of light, as if someone were using a flashlight to find their way around the clinic, glittered in the building's front window.

I straightened in my seat. "Did you see that?"

Maeve glanced out the car's back window. "It was probably the reflection of headlights from a car passing by. I didn't get a notification that anyone had disarmed the alarm system."

She had shown up when I'd disarmed the clinic for Buddy's emergency. Still, last I checked, cars didn't come with a stealth mode. We would have heard one pass behind us. "There was no car passing by." My mind ran through everything I'd done right before leaving the clinic. I'd been distracted. "I might have forgotten to arm the alarm system."

I unsnapped my seatbelt and leaned forward slightly, though those couple of extra inches weren't likely to give me any advantage. A movement of light in the window again, fainter this time as if they'd gone into the back, where the animals were kept.

I straightened. "There *is* someone in there."

I threw open the door.

Maeve jumped out of the other side of the car a second behind me. "You can't go in there. You're not some superhero. They might have a gun."

I skidded to a stop. I hadn't thought about what weapon they could be carrying, but they must have come prepared with some way to kill Buddy. The poison they'd used before would have been chosen because it was something they could sneak past Edith. They didn't have to be sneaky this time.

Maeve was right. They could as easily turn whatever weapon they'd brought with them on me. I'd have to hope I could convince them that that would be a bad idea because there was a difference in the eyes of the law between killing an animal and killing a person. "If we wait for the police, Buddy might already be dead by the time they get here."

"Oh for heaven's sake! If you're going to be reckless, at least take the tire iron with you."

I spun back around. She had the trunk open, tire iron in her hand.

It figured she would know exactly where it was.

I took the tire iron from her. "Call the police."

Maybe whoever was inside wasn't here to hurt Buddy or any of the animals, but they had broken into the building. That alone was a crime. We'd need the police one way or the other.

I sprinted for the front door and pulled it open. They must have picked the lock because the window was intact. What were the chances that the intruder wouldn't hear or wouldn't know what the door opening sounded like?

I slid to the left, toward the front desk and Maeve's office, so that I wasn't standing directly in line of sight from the back. The faint light of a computer screen shone softly from the office.

That was odd. Maeve was fastidious about not wasting energy. She wouldn't have accidentally left her computer on. I hadn't used the computer for the last-minute client because I'd been late. I'd planned to update the file tomorrow. Had the intruder been poking around for information on Maeve's computer, too? That didn't fit with someone here to hurt Buddy.

No one had come out of the door that led to the back. Hopefully that meant they hadn't heard me come in. I skirted along the wall until I was beside the door.

I raised up on my tiptoes and peeked through the window. Whoever was back there must have turned off their flashlight. Everything was dark. So much for the hope that they didn't know I was here.

If they had a gun and decided to shoot blind, I'd be safer if I stayed low.

I dropped to my hands and knees and crawled through the door. Crawling with one hand trying to keep the tire iron from clanking on the floor was a lot harder than I'd thought it would be. I had to stop twice to readjust my grip.

The faint green glow of the single nightlight we left plugged in for the animals gave the room an eerie swamp-monster horror-movie feel. The bars on the kennels had a stark prison look, and everything was angles and shadows.

My blood pounded in my ears. I'd come here to protect Buddy. Maybe I could get him and get out before the intruder knew I was here.

I wouldn't be able to carry him and the tire iron, though. I eased it to the ground. It clinked on the floor, and I flinched. Would I be lucky enough that the intruder would think that had been one of the natural noises a building made, like groaning pipes?

I inched toward Buddy. A form loomed up out of the darkness right beside me, something in their hands. My skin went cold and shivery. I should have listened to Maeve and waited outside for the police. Now Buddy and I were both going to die.

Not without a fight, though. I hadn't survived a childhood with Tonya only to die at the hands of someone else who put what they wanted above the lives and needs of anyone else.

Besides, they might shoot me, but if I could delay

them long enough, the police would get here in time to save Buddy and catch this person.

I launched myself at their legs. The impact knocked the air from my lungs. The intruder let out a very female scream and toppled backwards, limbs thrashing. The thing they'd been holding flew into the air and hit the ground with a heavy clank.

The intruder was woman, and now she was unarmed. I leaped on top of her the way I would straddle a large dog that didn't want to hold still to have its blood drawn. If I could restrain a Rottweiler, I should be able to hold this woman down.

An arm clocked me in the mouth, and the copper tang of blood hit my tongue. Pain burned through my cheek as if one of my teeth had cut the inside.

"Don't hurt me!" Kat's voice shrieked from underneath me. Hands continued to windmill in the air, and I leaned back to avoid taking another blow. "I was getting you what you asked for."

What the…? I wriggled off of the body beneath me. "Kat? What are you doing here?"

Kat stilled. "Zoe?"

For a brief second, I thought about saying, *No, it's her evil doppelganger.* But if Kat believed me, she might start trying to hit me again. "Maeve and I were driving by after the meeting"—that was only a tiny lie, right?—"and we saw a light on."

She hadn't asked me what I was doing here, but telling her should pave the way for her to answer my question. I felt my way backward to the wall by the door, climbed to my feet, and flicked on the light switch.

The bright fluorescent lights flooded the room in an industrial brightness, like we were in a showroom instead of a veterinary clinic. Kat blinked up at me from where she sat on the floor. A heavy-duty flashlight lay beside her, as did a few vials and a lot of pill containers.

Kat hadn't come here to harm Buddy the way I'd feared, but she still shouldn't have been here, walking around in the dark rather than turning on the lights—and with an armload of medication.

I narrowed my eyes at her. I'd look either fierce or crazed, but I'd settle for either right now. "What *are* you doing here?"

Tears rolled down Kat's cheeks. "Maeve's here too, you said? She's not going to forgive me the way Sebastian did." She reached a hand out toward me. "You have to explain it to her, and fight for me the way I fought for you."

She meant the way she fought to get me hired and then keep me after I was questioned about Sebastian's murder.

But this was a lot more serious than that. There'd been no evidence that I'd done anything wrong. Kat was sitting in the middle of a pile of medications that she'd clearly been intending to steal.

I pressed the heel of my hand briefly to my forehead. Of course. The computer in Maeve's office had been on, too. The strange discrepancies in the records. Those had to be Kat trying to cover her trail as well as she could.

And it sounded like Sebastian had known.

That was motive. If he'd decided to turn her in because she'd been stealing, she might have killed him to protect her secret.

My legs locked, stiff like they were made out of rusted metal instead of flesh. I'd suspected Maeve, but I'd never considered Kat. Could she have pretended all this time to be my friend, only to have killed Sebastian and allowed me to become the primary suspect?

Kat didn't move toward me, and she had no weapon, unless I wanted to count the clunky flashlight that looked like it was made out of plastic rather than metal. I probably wasn't in imminent danger from her, and I had to know the truth before the police got here. Detective MacIntosh might not tell me anything after he arrested Kat.

"I can't advocate for you unless I know everything." I tried to keep my voice calm and steady. It came out cold instead.

Kat brought her legs in to sit cross-legged. She scrubbed at the tears on her cheeks. "I had this...this skiing accident a couple years ago, and I tore up my knee. The painkillers they gave me in the hospital were so helpful. Once they took them away, I hurt all the time." She looked up at me with an expression that begged me to understand, to say that what she'd done wasn't so very bad, to say it could have happened to anyone. "But my doctor wouldn't give me more because they were a controlled substance. I found someone who would trade me some of what we carry in the clinic for the pills I needed."

Kat was an addict. I'd lived with an addict before. Should I have seen the signs? But Tonya hadn't been into prescription pain killers. The drugs she'd taken had been harder, and her symptoms were impossible to hide. Kat's only tells had been extra nervousness and a tendency to look like she hadn't slept. Which could as easily have been due to recent circumstances.

A siren wailed faintly in the distance. Almost out of time.

"Sebastian knew?" I asked.

If I'd had time to think about it, I could have come up with something more articulate or something that sounded less accusatory. But Kat seemed ready to spill everything. She might not be so willing once the police arrived and she was reminded of her right to remain silent. I could testify in court to whatever she told me now.

Kat bobbed her head. "He figured it out. I tried to hide it in the records." She shrugged as if she couldn't be expected to be the perfect criminal. "I begged him not to tell Maeve because she'd want to fire me. I promised him I'd get help, and I wouldn't steal anything else. He said I could have one more chance."

Sebastian said that? Maybe he'd grown up and changed in the years we'd been apart. I had. I was still me, but I wasn't the exact same person I'd been in college. Who would want to be a college-age maturity and have a college-age brain forever?

Sebastian might have changed. The thought felt strange in my mind, like running my tongue over a new filling in a tooth. Sebastian might not have been the same selfish liar I'd known.

Had I been too anxious to prove he'd died doing something bad? So convinced he'd been the kind of person who'd do something that would get him killed that I'd overlooked other possibilities? If Kat had killed him, he'd died trying to do something good. Trying to give someone a second chance. And that meant he wasn't the villain I'd made him out to be.

Well, not entirely, anyway.

The sirens grew louder.

Kat wouldn't risk attacking me with the police so close. I could pretty much get away with asking her anything at this point. "And he caught you stealing again. Did you poison him with something you'd stolen, or did you take one of the drugs we use for euthanasia?"

Kat's tears eased, as if I'd shocked them away. Her mouth hung open wide enough that I could have stuck her flashlight in it. "I didn't steal again. This was the first time since." The tears started again, faster, and she gulped a sob. "You think I killed him? I wouldn't. Never. I didn't."

"Police!" a man's voice shouted from the reception area.

I stepped away from the door. It flew back as if the officer had kicked it open. Good thing I'd moved.

Detective MacIntosh burst through. He had his gun out. "Hands up!"

Kat's hands flew up. I lifted mine more slowly. Surely he didn't mean me, too, but considering he'd once thought I'd killed Sebastian, it seemed better not to take the risk.

He cast me a considering glance, but he kept the gun trained on Kat. "Lower your hands, Dr. Stephenson. Maeve told me you're only in here because the two of you thought there was an intruder." He frowned and nodded his head toward Kat. "Doesn't she work here, too?"

His gun lowered slightly. Kat looked at me with puppy-dog eyes.

I could say this was all a misunderstanding. After all, whether she was prosecuted for stealing was up to Maeve, not me.

But if she had killed Sebastian...she claimed she hadn't had anything to do with it, yet she'd lied to both Maeve and me. Sebastian had lied to Maeve to cover up for Kat.

This was bigger than stealing. I couldn't be the one to decide what happened here. Maeve had said I wasn't a superhero. I also wasn't the police or a judge and jury.

I couldn't meet Kat's eyes. "Yes, she works here, but she was stealing prescription-only medications, and Sebastian caught her doing it before."

The words tasted bitter on the way out. I might as well have kicked her for the way Kat looked at me.

Was this how Keith felt when I'd basically called him a traitor and a sell-out? To Kat, it probably seemed like I'd stabbed her in the back to turn the attention off of myself.

Should I have lied for her? I'd lied for Tonya for years, and all it'd accomplished was to allow her to continue breaking the law and hurting people.

Detective MacIntosh ordered Kat to stand up and put her hands behind her back because she was being detained. He handcuffed her and led her out the door.

I glanced at the medicine scattered on the floor but left it where it was. It was evidence.

I dragged myself toward the front door slowly, giving Detective MacIntosh plenty of time to put Kat into the police cruiser before I followed them out. If this was the right thing to do, why did it feel like I'd screwed up yet again?

I exited through the front door. Maeve stood in the middle of the parking lot. The oscillating red and blue police lights cast her into a round of light and shadows that left her looking angry and terrified by turns.

She spun in my direction as if she'd heard my footsteps. "Why are they arresting Kat? If it was just her inside, then everything's fine. Ryan wouldn't tell me anything. This has to be a mistake, doesn't it?"

Everything that had happened, everything Kat had

told me, poured out like I was a balloon that had been popped with a dart.

Maeve's skin took on a gray cast by the time I was halfway through. When I finished, we stood staring at each other.

"So Sebastian's murder might be solved?" Maeve's voice sounded tiny, as if it was too much to hope for that this could all be over. "It wasn't someone from OABSL after all?"

She glanced back over her shoulder. Detective MacIntosh's squad car pulled out of the parking lot. He'd turned off his lights.

She wrapped a hand around her throat. "I don't know whether to hope she did kill him or she didn't."

The look on her face mirrored the one I was sure was on mine. That stunned, *this can't be happening* expression. "In some ways, life would be easier if she did, right? We wouldn't have to keep wondering what happened and why someone killed Sebastian. I wouldn't have to worry anymore that someone was trying to frame me for Sebastian's murder."

"But it's Kat." Maeve's tone was still hollowed-out and confused.

"But it's Kat," I repeated.

Kat, who'd helped us with fighting the breed ban. Kat, who'd been part of our group text, sharing funny stories about the people we'd encountered while stuffing fliers. Kat, who'd allowed Orion to get as much drool on her scrubs as he wanted, never pushing him away, even after he'd taken a big, slobbery drink of water. Kat, who'd helped me get and keep this job.

Kat, my friend.

"I thought she was my friend."

Did I say that? No, I'd heard the words audibly. They'd come from Maeve.

Kat, *our* friend.

I held open my arms in the universal invitation for a hug. Maeve hesitated for a breath and then walked in.

She wrapped her fists in the back of my shirt, holding on tight. Her breathing was ragged, and her body shook. She hadn't seemed like a woman grieving her fiancé before. Maybe she just hadn't felt like she could grieve when his case was still open, and she had so many pieces of her life to try to pick up. Maybe she'd felt trapped in a holding pattern while the police investigated.

Maybe it hadn't even felt real to her. Life could be like that sometimes. If you didn't look a tragedy in the face and you just kept moving, sometimes you could keep the grief from catching up to you. For a little while, at least. Grief always caught you in the end.

Maeve let me go and stepped back. She swiped her fingers under her eyes. It didn't help. Her mascara had run down her face, making her look like she was about the audition for a zombie movie. "Where's my tire iron?"

Grief apparently didn't cause her to forget details. "After all that, what you're worried about is your tire iron?"

"I can't do anything about that tonight." Maeve waved her hand in the direction the police car had gone, but her voice cracked slightly on the end. "But if I leave my tire iron behind and get a flat, that will be my own fault."

19

The lights were still on in the house when an officer drove me home, even though it was almost midnight. A figure of someone at the window sat like a dark cutout behind the gauzy lace curtains. Judith had waited up.

Maeve and I both had to give our statements at the police station. My phone still wasn't working, so I'd called Judith from Maeve's phone to tell her that the police might have caught Sebastian's killer and that I'd be home as soon as I could.

The door was unlocked. I left my hand on the knob without pushing the door open for almost twenty seconds. How was I supposed to tell Judith that it was Kat the police arrested tonight?

On the other side of the door, the soft whirring noise of Judith's wheels said she was moving toward me. I couldn't be a coward now. This was part of being a big sister, too. You heard the bad news first, and you tried to find a way to make it hurt a little less for your sibling.

I just didn't have any practice with it was all. Mom and Dad had always handled that part of our family life before. More Mom than Dad, actually. Dad's contribution was always more "Let me get your mom." He could help all his congregation through the worst things that came their way, but when it involved Judith and me, he was suddenly afraid of making it worse.

Maybe I took after him more than I'd realized.

"Zoe," Judith's voice said, "you're letting in mosquitoes."

I stepped inside and closed the door behind me, then bent down to take off my shoes, avoiding eye contact for as long as I possibly could. A mosquito buzzed around my ear as I did. Dang it. I had let in mosquitoes. That hadn't just been Judith's way of convincing me to come inside.

I set my second shoe aside.

Judith stared at me. "Is it that bad? Is it someone we know?"

"We know almost everyone in town in some capacity."

"You know what I mean."

The way she was looking at me, her eyes a little too wide and her lips open like she couldn't get enough air through her nose alone, flashed the truth at me like a spotlight. Bad news couldn't be softened. That was a lie the bearer of bad news tried to tell themselves to make the sharing easier on them, not on the person receiving the news.

I swallowed hard, but my throat still grated like it was made of sand paper. "It was Kat. They arrested Kat."

The rest of the story poured out. When I finished, we both moved to the living room.

I sank into our dad's recliner. The reclining part hadn't worked in years, so I tucked my legs up beside me instead and breathed in the scent of Old Spice that still lingered in the fabric. Grown woman or not, I could have used a hug from my dad right about now.

Judith looked blankly at the wall for long enough that I started to drift into that half-awake, half-asleep place where everything felt warm.

"It wasn't Kat."

I jerked upright. My tongue felt fuzzy and unwieldy, and the words wouldn't come.

Judith tapped a finger on the arm of her chair. "We all thought whoever killed Sebastian also tampered with my brakes. Kat wouldn't have tried to hurt me. We're friends."

It seemed like I was hearing that an awful lot tonight. Or thinking it. Like when Keith had voted against me without telling me. Like when I'd lashed out cruelly at him. "Friendship doesn't count for much sometimes."

Judith tilted her head to the side and pursed her lips. It was our mom's you-did-not-just-say-that look. "You know that's not true. Besides, even if I was a stranger,

Kat wouldn't have had any reason to want to hurt me. I didn't know about her stealing. I didn't see her in any suspicious situations. She didn't have access to the shelter's financials, and even if she did, we don't keep anything worth stealing on site."

Even my tired brain could follow her logic. "All that proves is that Kat didn't try to kill you. That doesn't prove she didn't kill Sebastian. Your accident must have been an accident after all."

Judith's face was determined. "What about Mayor Cameron's dog? Kat didn't poison Buddy."

"I could have been wrong that it was related, too. Dogs get into the trash all the time and eat things they shouldn't. Edith might have thrown out an aspirin, or a pack of gum containing xylitol, or old coffee beans, any of which could have made Buddy sick. She admitted he got into her trash. Just because she also blamed the 'pit bull people' doesn't make it true. She's the same woman who tried to force me to get a DNA test for Orion. She doesn't think straight when it comes to pit bull-type dogs thanks to her trauma as a child."

"That...makes sense." Judith slumped in her wheelchair like a marionette with her strings cut. "I should want you to be right so all the other things weren't attacks, but Kat killing Sebastian..."

She didn't have to finish. Sitting in the police station, all I'd been able to think about was what Sebastian must have been thinking when he figured out that someone he'd thought he could trust had poisoned him. Had he begged for his life? Had he tried to get help?

"The witness I talked to did say she saw a woman around Sebastian's house the night he died. Detective MacIntosh thought it was me. Originally, I'd suspected it was Maeve. Then when it couldn't be Maeve, I figured the witness was mistaken about what day she saw the woman there. Like maybe she saw me going into his house after Sebastian was already missing. But it must have been Kat."

Judith wrapped her arms around her torso. "I don't think I'm going to be able to believe it unless Kat confesses to killing Sebastian. She's not the kind of person who'd kill someone. Even if you're right about everything else, I still think someone from OABSL must have killed Sebastian." Judith's eyebrows lowered, and she glanced at the door. "Wait a second. Why did a police car bring you home? What happened to your car?"

***

I couldn't sleep, so I stayed up instead and baked a batch of cookies. I owed Keith an apology, and apologies always went over better if they came along with a gift.

I waited until it was a decent hour, packed up the cookies, and went next door to his house. I pushed the doorbell.

He opened the door. His gaze fell on me, and all expression wiped from his face. "Here to ask another favor?"

My skin turned sticky and tingly. I deserved that. In almost every conversation we'd had, I'd asked for something, or he'd helped me in some way. The one nice thing I'd done for him was bring cookies to thank him for saving Judith's life. And cookies every week for a year wouldn't have come close to paying him back for that.

None of that made it any easier. Apologizing when you knew you'd done something wrong should have been the easiest thing in the world. Cathartic. Instead, all I could hear was Tonya in my head reminding me of all the ways I didn't measure up.

My mouth was so dry that my tongue felt stiff. "Yes, I need another favor."

He crossed his arms over his chest and leaned his shoulder into the door frame. It wasn't a welcoming posture. It was resigned. Like he didn't expect anything better from me.

But he also wasn't turning me away. He was living Christ's instructions to walk the extra mile. Whatever I asked, he was probably going to actually try to help me with it, despite how I'd treated him.

"Well?" he said. "What is it?"

"I need..." I swallowed hard, but it didn't help. I shoved the box of cookies toward him. "I need you to forgive me. I was wrong. And after all you've done for us, you didn't deserve to be treated that way."

His gaze softened, and he pushed away from the door frame. "I didn't do it to hurt you or trick you, you know. I had to do what I thought was right."

I waved a hand in the air. He didn't owe me any explanations.

He accepted the box. "Is it expecting too much to hope these are cookies again?"

A smile curled my lips. "Peanut butter with chocolate chips this time. If you ever want more cookies, you just have to let me know. You're on our special cookies-for-life plan."

"Cookies for life, eh?" He smiled, and something inside my belly unfurled. "I could get used to that."

All my witty, flirty comebacks tangled up inside my head. Time to get out of here before I said something stupid instead. I held up a hand in farewell and turned to go.

"Zoe?"

I turned back.

Keith had the box of cookies stuffed under his arm and the other hand hooked into his pocket. "How about I take you to dinner for my apology?"

I rolled my eyes. "You don't have anything to apologize for. I was the one who acted like a spoiled brat."

His smile widened. "Then how about I just take you to dinner?"

Wait. Was that... "Are you asking me on a date?"

His face held an expectant expression. "I am."

Was this a joke? Hadn't he seen what a giant mess I was? An emotional time bomb. Not to mention all the things he didn't know about me that would ultimately end any relationship we started.

Not the least of which was... "My biological mother's in prison."

He raised an eyebrow. "Will she be joining us?"

Heat torched my face. It was a miracle my skin didn't burn off. He wasn't a stupid man. He should understand this without me having to explain it. "No, but if we go on a date, people are going to be sure you know about her. I wanted you to hear it from me first. In case you want to change your mind."

"Well, if anyone says anything to me about it, I'll tell them that the Bible's pretty clear. We're not judged for the actions of other people." His lips quirked up on one side. "Then I'll remind them what the Bible says about gossip."

I snorted. There were a lot of people in this town who weren't going to like that.

He leaned forward slightly. "So is that a yes?"

If he could handle the truth about Tonya, maybe he could handle the other things, too. And he was handsome. And kind. And he'd saved Judith's life. There wasn't a reason to say no. "That's a yes."

He motioned at the bench swing on his front porch. "Do you want to sit for a bit? I can get us coffee to go with these cookies, and we can decide where you'd like to go?"

I glanced at the loveseat-sized bench. Sitting there with him, with coffee and cookies, sounded like a much better way to spend the morning than what I needed to do. My shoulders slumped. "I can't. I have to go to the garage and find out what happened to my car."

***

Walking to the garage where Maeve had my car towed took over an hour. Being without both Judith's car and mine wasn't going to be sustainable long-term, even though Arbor had a walk-whenever-you-can culture. When we needed to see Judith's specialist in the city for her follow-up, I wasn't going to be able to push her wheelchair for three or more hours in ninety-degree weather.

Hopefully my car was a smaller repair. Her car had been a write-off. We were still waiting on the insurance company to send us a check so we could try to find her a replacement.

A couple of the pairs of people I passed along the way had Kat's name on their lips. In Arbor, secrets had a shorter shelf life than milk left on the counter in August.

The garage was the same one where I'd had a tire repaired a couple of times in high school when I ran over a nail. The main area was a warehouse-sized bay with two garage doors big enough to fit eighteen-wheelers. They left the doors open. Two cars were up on winches inside, one with men crawling around under it.

My car sat outside in the lot. When my phone had come back to life this morning for ten minutes, I'd had enough time to check my voicemails. Along with a message from the garage asking me to come in to talk about the repairs for my vehicle, there'd been another one from the lawyer handling my grandfather's estate. I'd been in the middle of writing down her number so I could call her back from Judith's phone when mine died again. Maybe my phone carrier would have a payment plan for a new phone. Who was I kidding? Any new phone was out of reach. I'd have to buy a used one online.

There was no door to knock on, so I walked into the bay and over to where the men were. "Excuse me?"

A man rolled out from underneath the car. He had red hair and a smattering of freckles across his nose. His baby-face cheeks suggested he wasn't long out of high school. "Yup?"

Yup? Customer service really was a thing of the past. "I'm Zoe Stephenson. I got a call this morning about my car."

"Yup."

Breathe in through my nose. Breathe out through my mouth. Don't take out the stress of the last few days on this kid. He was definitely not a man or he'd be able to string more than a word together in a sentence. "Can you tell me what's wrong with it?"

The kid looked up at me without so much as making a move to get off the lory or whatever the rolling thing he was on was called. "Nope. Didn't work on that one."

I gritted my teeth together so hard that my jaw ached. "Can you point me to someone who did?"

The other man who'd been under the car rolled out. "Stephenson. Is that the car that came in late last night?"

I was *not* going to lose my temper. I was not. No eruptions of Zoe the Volcano. I was not going to cover this place in ash like Vesuvius did Pompeii. But honestly, couldn't the other guy have spoken up when I first gave my name? "That's the one."

He rolled the rest of the way out and sat up. "Yer looking at a big bill for that one."

My stomach tightened. Great. Perfect. On top of a cell phone that wouldn't work, I was going to have a "big bill" for my car. Where was *that* money going to come from? Even the inheritance from my grandfather wasn't going to come in time, especially given my phone wouldn't stay on long enough for me to deal with it.

If I put off hearing exactly how much, would it magically go away, or did that tactic only work with monsters when you were a kid hiding under the covers? Maybe they had a payment plan so I could make installments each week after I got paid. "What's wrong with it?"

The man made a dismissive noise in his throat. "Ya put diesel in your gas engine."

What sounded like a snickering laugh came from under the car. If I hadn't just gotten out of trouble with the police, giving that kid's rolling thing a good kick and watching him fly across the room would be *really* satisfying.

"Ya can't put diesel in a gas engine." The man drawled his words. "Diesel fuel's got low octane so it can't combust properly. We gotta drain and clean yer whole fuel system."

Wait, what? They thought I'd put diesel in my fuel tank? My ears buzzed like they were still full of the mosquitoes from last night. I hadn't put diesel fuel in my car last time I filled up, accidentally or otherwise. I knew I hadn't, and not only because diesel fuel nozzles don't even properly fit in the slot on my car.

The last time I filled up my car, I'd been driving with Maeve to the police station to turn over the clinic's financial records. They'd been out of diesel fuel. I couldn't possibly have accidentally put diesel fuel in my car.

Besides, I'd driven my car to work yesterday morning because I'd planned to drive to the council meeting last night. My car ran fine on the drive to work. If there'd been diesel in it then, it would have quit before I arrived.

Which meant someone had to have intentionally added diesel fuel to my engine to prevent me from getting to the council meeting. While I was at work, someone had tampered with my car.

20

"You're sure that's why my car died?" I could still see the orange piece of paper taped to the gas station pump. *No Diesel*, it'd said. "Someone put diesel into my gas tank?"

Sounds like someone choking on a laugh came from under the car that was up on the winch. "The diesel gremlins did it."

Of course they wouldn't believe I hadn't done it. In their minds, I was like a child trying to hide a broken glass and claiming that they had no idea how it'd gotten broken in the first place. Or blaming it on the cat.

"Ma'am?"

The tone in the man's voice coming from behind me suggested it wasn't the first time he'd called for me. I turned around.

Unlike the two I'd been speaking to before, this man

was middle-aged and dressed in jeans and a flannel-patterned button-down shirt. And his hands were clean.

He held out a hand. "Barry Cameron. This is my place. You're the vet who's treating my dog, Buddy, right?"

So this was Edith's husband. They looked a bit mismatched, but who knew what Edith had been like before she became mayor. "That's right."

A smile split the man's face. His front teeth overlapped slightly. "Normally what your car needs we'd charge a couple grand for, but for you, it'll only be the cost of supplies. No charge for the labor. Buddy's like our second child. Edith would've been brokenhearted if anything happened to that little guy."

The inside of my nose tickled the way it did when tears were about to come if I didn't fight them back.

I'd been so focused on everything else, but that, right there, the way he looked when he talked about Buddy and his relief that he was going to be okay? That made my job worth every long day and grumpy client. That made coming back to Arbor worth it. "Thank you. And you're welcome."

He gave me a nod and then disappeared back into what was probably an air-conditioned office.

The sense of wellbeing that had flooded me at his kindness evaporated as soon as I headed back outside. As big a blessing as not having to pay the full amount was, it didn't fix that someone had done this to me intentionally.

I'd been stopped from attending the council meeting due to a mechanical failure in my car the same as Judith had—with less bodily harm. With Kat accused of Sebastian's murder, I'd been convinced Judith's crash was an accident after all, but that couldn't possibly be the case now.

Both of our cars dying on the way to a council meeting where the ban was being voted on was too big a coincidence.

By the time I walked back home, the temperature has risen into the asphalt-is-melting-and-sticking-to-the-bottom-of-my-shoes range.

Inside the house, Orion looked up at me from his spot on the floor, flopped his tail twice, and promptly went back to sleep. I flung myself down on my back into the couch, across from where Judith sat in her wheelchair, a pile of fabric in her lap.

Judith paused whatever she'd been listening to on her phone and pulled her earbuds out. "Uh-oh. That was definitely a flop. What's wrong?"

Where to start? That we were back to her accident maybe not being an accident. That someone had tampered with my car, too. That I was starting to doubt that Kat was guilty of murder. That the person who'd cut Judith's brakes might still be walking free.

I spilled it all out.

When I got to the part where someone must have put diesel into my gas tank, Judith gasped and stuck her finger in her mouth. "Jabbed myself."

I took a closer look at the blankets that were not only piled in her lap but also in a mound on the floor next to her. "What are you doing?"

"Mending torn blankets for the shelter." The words came out in a mumble around her finger.

"Since when did you learn to sew?"

"I didn't." Judith removed her finger and squinted at it as if she couldn't figure out how a wound too small to draw blood could hurt so much. "But I figured now was as good a time as any to learn. I've been watching videos online, and the dogs won't care if my mending looks like it was done by a one-handed drunk." She held up the needle she'd dropped. The thread had fallen out. She sagged. "I just wish the hole at the end wasn't so small and hard to get the thread through. No one's eyesight is that good."

Was she deliberately avoiding responding to what I'd told her? Judith tended to be a slow cooker when it came to responding to things, but she seemed completely absorbed in threading her needle.

I squirmed in my chair. "So what do you think? Could Kat actually be innocent of Sebastian's murder?"

Judith's tongue was now sticking out between her lips as she concentrated. She licked the end of the thread again. "I said she was all along. She didn't have any reason to cut my brake lines."

I grabbed a pillow and squished. Hard. "The OABSL didn't have a reason to keep me from the council meeting. We weren't exactly subtle. We spoke to every town councilor. We canvassed the town. We made it obvious on purpose where we stood on the mayor's ban."

Judith glanced up at me. "If you squeeze that any harder, the stuffing's going to come out, and I'm going to need to sew about a hundred more dog blankets before I graduate to pillows."

I tossed the pillow to the floor. "If it wasn't someone from the OABSL behind everything, and it wasn't Kat, then I don't know who could have done all this."

Judith set her sewing down in her lap and looked up at me. "Maybe you're not the one who needs to figure it out." Her words were soft and her expression tentative. "I've had to make peace with the fact that I might never know if my crash was an accident or not. I think you need to do the same."

It was her I'm-right-but-I'm-afraid-you're-going-to-blow-up-when-I-tell-you voice. The too-calm voice. The mom voice.

I huffed out a breath, picked the pillow back up, and covered my face with it. *Repeat after me: You are a veterinarian, not a police detective.*

Detective MacIntosh was supposed to be the one figuring it all out. But his evidence all led to Kat. His evidence didn't protect Judith. Or me. Or Edith's Buddy.

Assuming all of this was connected somehow, the person who was behind it hadn't stopped. My car was only the latest and the least in a long line of casualties.

I peeked over the top of my pillow. Judith had the

needle and thread held up so close to her face that her eyes were practically crossed.

"I just want you to be safe."

Judith lowered the needle. "No one's tried to hurt me since my accident. They could have. I've been in this house alone and vulnerable while you were working and grocery shopping and walking Orion."

So at the very least, even if Judith's crash was intentional, the person who'd done it no longer saw her as a threat. "What about my car?"

"It could have been teenagers pulling a prank, the same as they sometimes smash mailboxes the night before Halloween. But think about it. Even if it wasn't a teenage prank, they're de-escalating. They made your car stop, but not in a dangerous way."

I sucked in a breath until my lungs ached with the stretch and let it slowly out. My car's demise was different from all the other events. I'd been safe the whole time. The person who'd done it hadn't wanted to hurt me.

Maybe it was time for me to back off and leave the investigating to the police.

But would that be abandoning Kat to a fate she didn't deserve?

21

The résumés submitted by people applying for the vet tech job blurred together in front of me. How was I supposed to decide whether five years' work experience was better than four years' work experience and a year teaching? Or whether someone applying from a big clinic in the city would be a better fit for us than someone who currently worked in a smaller clinic in a town more like Arbor? They all sounded good on paper. Maeve couldn't seriously expect me to narrow it down to three people we'd invite for interviews.

I shoved the pages into a pile and glanced back over my shoulder at where Maeve still sat at the computer, putting in an order for supplies. "You know that reviewing résumés isn't part of my job description, right?"

Maeve checked her handwritten note and then

typed something else into the computer. "It is if you want to become a partner in this business."

I twitched in my chair, and it threatened to roll me across the floor and into Maeve. "Partner? As in I'd own the business with you?"

"That's traditionally what that means. I have a business and management degree, not one in veterinary medicine. I shouldn't be running this place alone."

She didn't even stop what she was doing. Her reference was so off-handed that it was like we'd been discussing it previously. I was sure that wasn't a conversation I'd somehow missed.

Being a part-owner in a veterinary clinic in Arbor—that'd been my dream since high school. The one I'd thought was gone forever. And now Maeve was offering to hand it back to me—or, more specifically, offering me a chance to buy it back.

Which I might be able to do, depending on what my grandfather left me. I'd finally gotten through to the law firm handling his estate, and the receptionist booked a virtual appointment for me with the lawyer next week.

I didn't have much in the way of savings because of—

Crap. I didn't have much in the way of savings because I'd been unemployed for months after being fired from my previous job. If Maeve ever found out why I'd been fired, she wouldn't want me working for her, let alone being her business partner.

In some ways, Kat and I weren't so very different.

We'd both made bad choices and done things we shouldn't. Things we now regretted.

I spread the papers back out in front of me as if I were taking a closer look at them. "Do you think you'd hire Kat back if it turns out she stole from you but didn't kill Sebastian? We could speak on her behalf at her sentencing and ask the judge to give her probation."

I tried to keep my tone light and casual.

Maeve doubled clicked with her mouse. "You just don't want to look through any more résumés."

There was laugh in her voice, like she really thought that was the reason I'd asked about Kat.

True, I'd rather we could keep Kat on and give her one last chance. But that wasn't all of it. If Maeve couldn't move past what Kat did, then I couldn't consider becoming part of this business permanently. The truth would surface eventually. It always did.

I turned my chair around so that I was facing her back. "Seriously, though. Would you?"

The printer started spitting out papers, and Maeve wheeled her own chair around so that we were face-to-face. The smile was gone from her lips. "I don't know. Kat lied to me, and she convinced Sebastian to lie to me. Those aren't easy things to get over."

Being lied to was never easy to get over. It not only called into question everything a person would say to you in the future, but it made you doubt everything they'd said and done in the past. The safety was gone from the relationship.

If it was only about lying, then perhaps I could still have a chance here, assuming I could find the courage to confess my past to Maeve. If it was about the lying rather than the stealing, there was still hope.

"I think Kat was scared that if she told you, you'd fire her. She did tell Sebastian."

Maeve leaned back in her chair and rolled her eyes. "After he caught her."

My mouth was dry and my stomach tight, as if I were preparing to get the results of a potentially serious medical test. "My point is that she might not have thought she was lying to you since she didn't tell you to your face that she hadn't stolen anything. And she stopped stealing once Sebastian caught her. Until last night."

Maeve rubbed a knuckle across her lips. The angles of her face seemed to have softened. "How do we even know that's the truth?"

For once, her question didn't seem rhetorical. She was thinking this through. Kat might or might not be convicted of Sebastian's murder, but if she wasn't, I might be securing both our jobs. If I could show that she deserved another chance, a fresh start, then surely I deserved one, too.

First, though, I had to prove that Kat hadn't been lying, even though she hadn't told Maeve about her stealing from the start. "Kat said that she stopped stealing when Sebastian caught her. Could you check the files? You noticed something wasn't right when she was stealing, so you should be able to figure out when she stopped."

Maeve's chair rocked back and forth, then spun back to face the computer. "You know this is ridiculous, don't you? It won't change the fact that she's in jail right now for killing Sebastian."

The air sucked out of my lungs, like I'd stepped into a giant vacuum. All I'd been thinking about was showing that Kat hadn't been as deceptive as Maeve thought she was. But if I was right, didn't that also prove more?

"It might, though." My words came out a little too high and a little too fast. "It might change everything. If Kat was telling the truth about stopping once Sebastian caught her, then she doesn't have a motive for killing him."

Maeve's hand stilled on the mouse, and she shot a sideways glance at me. "Go on."

I bounced in my seat, pulling one leg up and tucking my ankle under the opposite thigh. "Detective MacIntosh thinks Sebastian caught Kat stealing again after he warned her to stop, or that she might have been lying about him giving her a second chance." I waved a hand in the air. "Doesn't matter which. The important part is that if we can show that the thefts stopped before Sebastian was murdered and didn't pick up again after he was murdered—"

"Until the night of the council meeting."

I rolled my chair to beside hers. "That was weeks

later. If she killed him to cover up for her thefts, then she'd have had no reason to stop after killing him. She could have continued to get away with it."

"Theoretically." Maeve clicked on a few icons, and spreadsheets and old order forms filled the screen. "Now be quiet and let me do the math."

22

Maeve and I stared at the highlighted and notated stacks of sheets. The air conditioner clicked on again, and I jumped. I glanced at the clock. We'd been sitting in silence for nearly five minutes.

Maeve tapped her capped highlighter on the final sheet. "Does it all match? I'm not imagining things, am I?"

I shook my head. According to everything we'd found, the discrepancies that Maeve confronted Sebastian about stopped one week before she confronted him, which was a full month before his murder, and didn't start up again. Kat had been telling the truth. She hadn't only stopped stealing until Sebastian died. She'd stopped stealing from the clinic entirely.

Detective MacIntosh was wrong about her motive.

Maeve dropped the highlighter on the paper in a

way that reminded me of someone miming dropping a microphone. "Do you think it'll matter if we take this to the police? Will they actually consider it?"

It should matter. The truth *should* matter, whether it was inconvenient or not. Whether people liked it or not.

"There's only one way to find out." I stood up and collected the papers into a pile. "If we take them to the police now, there's a chance they'll let Kat go, and she won't need a bail hearing."

Maeve glanced at her watch. "It's already 6:30 pm. I'm supposed to be babysitting my niece in a half hour, and it takes that long to drive there."

Maeve had written all over the papers. Anyone reading them could clearly see exactly when the thefts started and stopped. Before, we'd only taken Detective MacIntosh the paperwork from the time when Kat was actively stealing. At the time, that'd seemed like the important part. "I'll take it."

Maeve swept all her belongings into her purse. "Call me if he has any questions. I have Bluetooth in my car."

I snapped my heels together and saluted.

She shot me a death glare and headed out to her car. "Hurry up if you want a ride there. I don't have time to dawdle."

***

Maeve was running late enough that she didn't even have time to park to let me out. She stopped in the street in front of the police station, and I hopped out.

The woman at the desk was a woman who knew my

mom rather than the one who hadn't wanted to let Maeve and me see Detective MacIntosh when we'd brought in the initial financial files.

I set my bulging brown envelope down on the counter. For some reason, standing here was like being called to the principal's office to defend myself for something I hadn't actually taken part in. "I have some information for Detective MacIntosh about one of the cases he's working on."

"I'm sorry, darlin'." She had a very soft Southern twang to her speech. "Shift change was a half hour ago, and I doubt he's still here."

She hesitated slightly on the last part, as if she couldn't be entirely sure it was true. Was Detective MacIntosh the kind of man who often stayed late to do paperwork? He'd seemed conscientious, even to the point of digging into Tonya's history and using it against me.

I leaned a little closer to the desk. "Could you check for me? It's important."

She shook her head. "That man works too hard as it is. I'm not asking him to stay even later. Not even for you, no matter who your mama is." She slid a hand toward the envelope. "You could leave this for him, and I'll make sure it gets onto his desk, if you'd like."

I snatched it back to my chest. He could too easily mistake these papers for the ones he'd already seen. Maeve's notes only explained things if you knew to look for them. "I'll come back tomorrow. I need to talk to him about it."

I headed out the front door. The parking lot was to the side. A few unused cruisers were parked at the back, but the body of the lot held the cars of the employees still in the building. If I was right that Detective MacIntosh was still inside, he'd eventually come to the parking lot for his car, assuming he hadn't walked to work, but most of the police force didn't. They needed to be able to get around quickly, even while off duty.

Sticking around wouldn't cost me anything other than a little time. I leaned against the building to wait.

Finally, a man came out of the side employees' door. Detective MacIntosh. His suit jacket was slung over his arm, and he'd loosened his tie and unbuttoned the top button of his dress shirt. Something about his posture made my chest ache. The slow way he walked spoke more to defeat than to exhaustion.

Maybe I should leave him be.

I straightened my spine. No, this was his job. He had to face everything that meant, good days and bad, the same as I had to handle the days where a client accused me of not caring about their animal in exchange for the days when a client baked me cookies. I had to handle the days when I lost a patient in exchange for the days when I saved what seemed like a hopeless case.

I did my job, and he needed to as well. Kat's whole future hung in the balance.

I raised a hand. "Detective MacIntosh!"

His shoulders went back, and it was like he slid a mask over his face. All genuine emotion vanished.

"Dr. Stephenson. You're on your own today?" He looked left and then right. "Where's your partner in..." A muscle twitched in his cheek.

He did not. He really was off his game. A snicker slipped out. "Were you about to ask me where my partner in crime was?"

My snicker grew into a belly laugh. Just thinking about him finishing the sentence fed into a tsunami-level force that I couldn't contain. Considering he'd actually thought Maeve and I were conspirators in Sebastian's murder at one point, it seemed like the most awkward thing he could have come up with.

He cleared his throat. "I could still arrest you, you know."

I took a deep breath, but the giggles came back. "For what? I didn't go to law school, but I'm pretty sure laughing at a police officer isn't a crime."

A touch of pink colored the top of his ears. That hint of humanity made him even more handsome. Too bad he didn't have a personality to match.

He crossed his arms over his chest. "Did you have a reason for accosting me in the parking lot other than to mock me?"

I swallowed and pressed a hand to my stomach. Not a good idea to antagonize him more.

I held the file out to him. "Maeve and I..." My cheeks pulled up into a grin. Nope. Do not laugh again. Hold it together. "We realized the financial information we gave you before was incomplete."

I explained everything. He watched me the whole time. When I finished, I extended the file again. "We're hoping you'll consider re-opening the case."

Detective MacIntosh drew in a long breath and let it out slowly. "I would have thought you'd be glad I wasn't looking at you for the murder anymore."

Shaking the file at him probably wouldn't get him to take it from me any faster, would it? It was especially tempting though. "Not when you arrested someone else who's also innocent." I couldn't help myself. I gave the file a little shake. Shaking things at people worked for Maeve. "Which you'll see as soon as you look at this."

"All that means is that she was cautious. It doesn't mean she didn't have motive. The rest of the evidence doesn't point to her innocence."

He stepped around me and strode toward a nearby car.

Not acceptable. He didn't get to brush me off like that. I sprinted after him, dodged past, and plastered myself across the driver's side door.

Detective MacIntosh froze, and his mouth dipped open slightly. "Did your parents give you any boundaries as a kid, or did you just have everything dropped in your lap whenever you wanted it if you whined long enough?"

The words hit me in the chest, and I sucked in a breath. My eyes burned. How. Dare. He.

"You know absolutely nothing about my life or my parents. There aren't better parents on the planet. I know because for years I had the exact opposite. And there's nothing wrong with being determined and fighting for what's right."

My hand tingled with the urge to slap him. But not only was hitting people wrong, he'd probably love to arrest me for assaulting a police officer.

Something I couldn't decipher flickered across his face, and he put a hand to the back of his neck and held it there. His posture slumped slightly. "I'll take a look, but I'm not promising anything. We have a solid case against Katherine Hardy. Along with motive, she had means. She was stealing medications, and hemlock is an ingredient in medications for things like bronchitis, swollen joints, epilepsy, and reversing strychnine poisoning."

The fire in my throat eased slightly. Not an apology, but maybe he recognized he'd crossed a line and this was as close as he could get to admitting it. He'd also accidentally told me something I hadn't known before. Sebastian died of hemlock poisoning.

Detective MacIntosh raised an eyebrow. "Are you going to give me whatever's in that envelope, or do I have to beg?"

I passed it over to him. "Are any of those medications that contain hemlock ones Kat actually had access to? We don't carry human medications, and I don't think hemlock is used as frequently in veterinary medicine."

He gave me a flat stare. "You don't know when to quit, do you?"

He was a grump. Fine. You didn't fight fire with fire. All that ever did was burn everything down. If you wanted to win, you fought fire with water.

I gave him my cheekiest grin. "Not when it's important. Quitters aren't survivors."

He made a motion for me to move out of the way. Since the papers we'd printed off were now tucked under his arm, I did.

He climbed into his car. "Goodnight, Dr. Stephenson. I'd say it was good seeing you again but..."

Was that a smile I heard in his voice? I bent down slightly so he could see me through the window. "Goodnight, Detective MacIntosh." I grinned at him. "Hopefully I don't see you again soon."

23

Detective MacIntosh's taillights vanished around the corner. The heat and humidity had eased off, but the sky wasn't changing shades yet. I should have plenty of time to walk home before the mosquitoes came out.

My purse vibrated slightly against my side. I pressed a hand against it. Had my phone come back to life?

I unzipped my purse and pulled my phone out. Maeve's name and number came up on the screen.

I swiped to answer.

"Are you already at home?" Maeve said, skipping any pleasantries.

I switched my phone to my right hand where it'd be more comfortable to hold. "No. I just finished giving the papers to Detective MacIntosh."

"Oh thank goodness." A child's voice called for Auntie Maeve in the background, and Maeve said something I couldn't catch, as if she'd covered the phone with her hand for a second. "Edith called me on my cell phone because she wants to pick up Buddy." Her voice had a harried tone, like she couldn't believe someone would do that.

I peeked at the time on my phone. "Does she realize we closed hours ago?"

"Oh, she knows. She called my cell phone, remember?" Maeve huffed. "She just doesn't care. Is he ready to go?"

Buddy had been ready to go for a while now. It'd only been Edith's overabundance of caution that required him to stay as long as he had. "Past ready."

Maeve said she'd call Edith back and give her a time to meet me there, taking into account that I'd be walking back. With all the walking—intentional and unintentional—that I'd done since coming to Arbor, I was bound to lose a few pounds—there were upsides to almost everything.

The parking lot was still empty when I got back to the clinic, even though it was only five minutes before the time Maeve said she'd tell Edith to be there. I disarmed the alarm system, went inside, and turned the computer back on.

I dropped into the computer chair. If I had to wait for Edith, I might as well make good use of my time. I pulled out the list Maeve and I had made of the medications Kat had stolen since the beginning.

The list wasn't long. Most of the medications she'd

stolen were painkillers, plus a few antibiotics. I knew by looking at most of them that they didn't contain hemlock. There were only two I wasn't sure of—a steroid and a de-wormer.

I double-checked that Maeve had correctly listed the de-wormer, but she had. Who would want to buy a de-wormer on the black market? There had to be an off-label use for it that I wasn't aware of.

I typed the name of the steroid into the Internet search bar and pulled up the product information. No hemlock. My search on the de-wormer yielded the same result.

Detective MacIntosh was going to hit a dead end when he tried to prove that Kat had used something she'd stolen from the clinic to poison Sebastian.

I could almost hear his voice. *Just because she didn't steal anything with hemlock outright doesn't mean she didn't take just enough of a medication with hemlock in it to poison Sebastian Clunes.*

Hopefully he'd at least seriously consider the information I'd passed along to him.

I rolled my chair to the office door and leaned out until I could see out the glass front door. Still no Edith. For someone who'd been so anxious to pick her dog up that she had me come back in after hours, you'd have thought she would at least be prompt. Good thing I didn't have anywhere else to be.

I wheeled myself back to the computer.

Detective MacIntosh might not believe in Kat's innocence, but I still did. His theory about why and how she'd killed Sebastian had too many holes. So, assuming that Kat hadn't stolen medication to poison Sebastian with hemlock, someone else must have gotten hemlock somewhere else.

I typed *hemlock poisoning* into the search bar and clicked on the first link.

Hemlock caused trembling, increased salivation, dilated pupils, muscle weakness, and convulsions. A shiver ran from my cheeks down through the rest of my body. I didn't want to know anymore. It was too easy to imagine what Sebastian's final moments had been like. I scrolled away from the symptoms list.

Besides, the symptoms wouldn't help me catch whoever did this to him. I needed something concrete and practical.

Hemlock had no antidote, the information said. Short of vomiting up the hemlock, having their stomach pumped, or not being given enough for it to be fatal, people didn't survive hemlock poisoning. Whoever had done this to Sebastian hadn't wanted to risk that he'd survive.

I scrolled further down the page. Symptoms could take thirty minutes to hours to manifest, so Sebastian might not have gotten confused and wandered out of his house, looking for help, at all. The fact that his body was found in the woods behind his house had never made sense to me. If he needed help, he should have gone out the front door or to one of the neighbors. But if he ingested the hemlock, went for a walk, and got sick while he was out, he could have been too sick to make it back home, or too disoriented to call for help or in an area where he couldn't get a clear enough cell signal.

I pressed the heels of my hands to my eyes. I didn't want to focus on that, either. The way Sebastian had treated me years ago was wrong, but he didn't deserve this kind of death, alone and suffering.

I had to focus. I couldn't bring Sebastian back. All I could do was make sure the right person was punished for it.

The most important question seemed to be how someone could get ahold of hemlock. The page said that it was a plant that grew everywhere in the United States, often mixed in with innocent plants. Sometimes people mistook the leaves for parsley or the root for parsnips and ate it by accident.

"Dr. Stephenson?" Edith's voice called from the waiting room.

I clicked over to the patient records, so that I could properly discharge Buddy.

Edith wore her Indiana Jane outfit again—tall rubber boots and a floppy brimmed hat. Her walking stick was absent, but presumably she left that in the car. "I'm sorry I'm late. Lateness is unforgivably rude. It took me longer than I thought to walk back to my car."

All my angry thoughts about her keeping me waiting softened at the edges. At least she acknowledged her behavior, which was more than could be said for certain other people, like Detective MacIntosh. "I'll get Buddy for you."

She handed me a leash. I collected him from the back. For such a little dog, he practically pulled my arm from my socket in his haste to get to Edith and then he wriggled around her legs, licking randomly at her boots.

She smiled indulgently down at him. She scooped him up. His tongue lapped the air, trying to hit her face and missing. "Are you sure he's ready to go? We take long hikes together. They haven't been the same without him."

Buddy had more energy than many patients who'd come in for their yearly exam and vaccinations. "Absolutely, but we do need to talk about what he might have eaten to make him sick. It's important for protecting him in the future. He was lucky this time, but next time might be fatal."

She waved a hand in the air as if to wipe my words away. "It won't happen again."

For someone who loved her dog so much, she was rather flippant. A plan for going home was part of my job. She didn't realize how many animals who did things like eat plastic came back in worse condition if their owners didn't take preventative measures seriously.

How could I impress the importance of this on her? I rubbed my knuckle with my forefinger. Maybe it was that she thought the circumstances were unique and couldn't happen again. "You said when you first brought him in that the pit bull people caused this, but—"

"I said no such thing." The smile Edith had been directing at Buddy shifted into a glare at me. "You must be thinking about someone else."

I frowned. I'd been sure she'd said that this was all the fault of "those pit bull people." Her statement was what made me think they'd been targeting people they assumed supported the breed ban. No *way* had I gotten that wrong.

Edith's face was firm. Her gaze didn't twitch away. Her mouth didn't move. She was apparently as certain as I was.

She had been under a lot of stress, afraid that Buddy was going to die. She probably hadn't been thinking straight. Obviously, she hadn't meant it, or she had been willing to blame anyone and everyone and now had forgotten what she'd said.

Fine. No need to push it if she realized her mistake. I'd already decided that Buddy had eaten something he shouldn't have from their garbage. That part I was certain of. Edith had definitely said he might have gotten into the garbage. If I didn't have to convince her that he hadn't been intentionally poisoned, we could move on to the important part.

"You mentioned that he got into the kitchen garbage. That's pretty common, and a lot of what people eat isn't safe for dogs. I know baby locks are ugly and a little inconvenient, but they do work."

I smiled at her, but she didn't smile back.

She tapped her foot on the floor. "No, I'm sure I

didn't say that, either. Perhaps you need to take better patient notes. While I appreciate you discharging Buddy after hours, I don't really have time to stand around and talk." She directed a pointed stare at the desk where the credit card machine lay.

Nope. She did not get to steamroll me about this. Buddy was *my* patient. I'd give her the benefit of the doubt that my memory had holes. It was possible. I hadn't taken a lot of notes that night. But we were going to discuss safety procedures. "This is part of the discharge process. We need to talk about Buddy's ongoing care. Where do you keep your household cleaners?"

She lifted her eyebrows, so high they nearly disappeared under her bangs. "We have a young child. We keep them locked up like any responsible parents should."

A basket of angry words bubbled up in my throat. This was for her dog's safety. Could she not find a minute to take this seriously?

She shifted her weight, and her boots squeaked. It seemed like an oddly uncomfortable gesture. It gave me an idea.

"What about on your walks? Does Buddy ever nibble on things along the way?" I tried to keep my voice light and neutral. She might be feeling awkward because she accidentally let him eat something and now blamed herself. She'd said he hadn't eaten any houseplants—I was absolutely certain of that since she told me he wasn't a cow—but I hadn't asked about outdoor plants. "Dogs are omnivores, so it's normal for them to try things you wouldn't expect."

A muscle in her cheek twitched as if she'd clenched her teeth. "He didn't eat anything along our walk. I was a Girl Scout. I know poisonous plants." Her words tumbled out a bit too fast, and she strode over to the counter and tapped her nails on it. "I think you're right. I do remember him getting into our garbage. I'm sure I overreacted about it, and he didn't even eat anything problematic. Or he ate a potato from the leftover stew I'd thrown out."

My back tensed. What was going on here? She wasn't exactly falling apart, but she was acting more nervous than I'd ever seen her. "Cooked potatoes aren't poisonous to dogs." The words came out automatically before I could stop them.

"Then some onion." She waved her credit card at me. "Are you going to allow me to pay, or has Buddy's stay been complimentary?"

My limbs moved robotically as I gave her the total and printed off her invoice. Something itched at my mind, and I couldn't reach it to scratch.

Edith left with nothing more than a perfunctory wave of her hand. She'd been edgy from the start of my questioning about what Buddy might have gotten into. Yet she'd been convinced enough at the time that she'd called the Pet Poison Help Line. She'd persuaded them enough that they'd instructed her to purge his stomach. So why deny or minimize it now?

I went back to the computer in the office, updated Buddy's file, and closed the program. The website I'd been reading on hemlock filled the screen again.

The air left my body in a rush, as if I'd been hit hard in the stomach.

Edith had gotten nervous when I'd talked about what Buddy could have gotten into. She hadn't wanted me to ask too many questions about the plants on their walk, and then she'd offered up that he'd eaten something from their garbage, probably thinking that would be the end of it. What if there was some truth in all of that?

My body went limp, like all the bones had vanished. The website said people ate hemlock by accident because the leaves looked like parsley and the root looked like parsnips. That meant hemlock could be hidden within food easily. Both parts could have been added to a stew or a soup and given to Sebastian to eat. He didn't lock his door. Edith could have gone in afterward and removed whatever takeaway dish she'd brought it to him in. Edith could have been the woman Sebastian's neighbor saw around his house the night he died.

And her husband ran a garage. Which didn't necessarily mean Edith knew how to cut brake lines, but it meant she might have access to the knowledge.

I'd thought this had to do with the confiscated pit

bull and the breed ban, and I'd been right. I'd just been looking in the wrong direction.

Sebastian and Judith weren't attacked because of the role they'd played in confiscating and rehoming Tim Gilpin's pit bull. They were attacked because they were intent on overturning the breed ban so that a similar situation wouldn't happen again.

If Edith were behind it all, that even explained how diesel fuel ended up in my gas tank. She'd wanted to stop me, too, but couldn't bring herself to kill me after I'd helped Buddy. Or perhaps her motives weren't even that quasi-noble. Maybe she'd been concerned about Buddy being taken care of if she'd killed me.

It all fit. Even why she'd panicked and called the Pet Poison Help Line. She knew exactly what Buddy had eaten and how deadly it could be.

I shut down the computer and turned off the lights. Detective MacIntosh wouldn't listen to me without something more concrete than "she can't explain how her dog got sick."

I needed proof.

24

"If I didn't know you better," Judith slid the bowl of fruit toward me across the breakfast table, "I'd say you had an unrequited crush on someone with the way you've been moping about. But you have a date soon with Keith, so that can't be it."

I piled fruit onto my yogurt and swirled it around. "What I wouldn't give for mom to be home and baking us carrot cake pancakes right now."

Our mom used to say that no problem couldn't be solved if you had a stomach full of pancakes. Though, in those days, our problems were more along the lines of struggles in math for Judith and failed driving tests for me, not murder suspects running free.

Judith stared at me, her eyes a little too wide and a piece of peach poised on her fork halfway to her mouth. "I was kidding, but is this about a guy?"

I snorted. "I wish."

Somehow risking a broken heart even seemed like an easier problem than this. How was I supposed to live in this town and see Edith on the street, knowing what she'd done but being unable to prove it?

Judith looked down at her bowl. "Are you feeling weird about liking Keith? It's okay for you to move on, you know. Maybe now that Sebastian's gone, it'll be easier."

My bite of yogurt went down the wrong way, and I coughed. My jaw seized, and my face went hot. "I *have* moved on. I've dated people since Sebastian."

"Never for longer than a couple of months."

That had absolutely nothing to do with Sebastian. Those guys had red flags, and I wasn't going to ignore red flags the way I did with Sebastian. I'd learned my lesson now. I was savvier.

But if I said that to Judith, she'd only say that I'd broken up with those guys at the first sign that they weren't perfect. She'd say my reasons only proved her hypothesis. That I had a Sebastian-shaped hole in my heart that I'd never allowed to heal, or some such nonsense like that.

There was no use arguing with someone who was wrong and wouldn't ever admit they were wrong.

I pushed my half-finished bowl away. "I'm going to take Orion for a walk and see if the cell phone guy has any refurbished phones for sale for cheap." I motioned toward the breakfast stuff on the table. "Don't worry about this. I'll clean it up when I get back."

"You can finish your breakfast, Zo," Judith's voice was soft. "I'll drop the subject."

My eyes burned. Which was stupid. This wasn't anything to cry about. Crying wouldn't change history or bring Sebastian back. "It's not that. I just need a working phone. I can't keep taking your phone when I'm on call, and we have that virtual meeting with the lawyer about Grandpa's estate next week, remember?"

I grabbed Orion's leash and my purse and scurried out the door.

***

The cell phone guy sold me a "gently used" phone and swapped the SIM card for me. It was an older model than the one Orion used as a chew toy, but at least it stayed on and held a signal. Functional was much more important than new. Functional and frugal, since Maeve certainly wasn't going to give me half the business for free.

I stepped out of the shop and sent Judith a text to tell her the mission was a success. I added an extra toothy smiley face and a couple of heart emojis. Hopefully she'd realize I wasn't angry at her.

Across the street, Edith and Buddy walked in the opposite direction from where Orion and I were headed. She wore her overly large floppy hat and purple boots and carried her walking stick. Buddy bounced along beside her as if his feet had springs. The lack of walks had probably been the most difficult part of his stay at the vet clinic. Edith seemed to walk him almost every day.

Orion stopped and scratched himself in the face with a back foot. I nearly tripped over him. Their walks in the woods. I should have thought of it before.

Edith would have likely collected the hemlock she used to poison Sebastian during their walks. Seeing it alongside their path might have even been what gave her the idea in the first place. She'd implied she was an experienced hiker who knew all about poisonous plants. She would recognize hemlock for what it was.

Maybe if I walked the path Edith always took, I could find a spot where she'd dug up the hemlock. It'd be circumstantial evidence at best, but perhaps it would be enough to convince Detective MacIntosh to consider the possibility.

I pivoted around. Orion gave me a look that clearly said *I wasn't done scratching here*. But we couldn't delay. The woods around Arbor were so full of hiking trails there'd be no way to guess which one Edith normally took aside from following her.

I stayed on the far side of the road so she wouldn't know she was being followed until she entered a trailhead and disappeared into the trees.

Orion and I jogged across the road, my gait awkward from trying to run in flip-flops. Why was it that I never had on appropriate footwear when I needed it? The sleuths in TV shows never had this problem. Then again, they seemed to think it was normal to run in boots with three-inch heels. No one could actually fight crime in heels.

The sign at the trailhead pointed out the two potential loops for hikers. One was two miles, and the other was five. I glanced down at my feet. The toe piece on my left flip-flop was already threating to pull free. I'd have to take the short trail today and come back with better footwear for the long one if I didn't find anything.

This path wasn't one of the more popular ones for vacationers. The trail didn't offer a view of the water at any point, and there was a patch that got borderline swampy when it rained. The campers and hikers who flooded into the area around Arbor during the warmer months tended to stick to the more interesting, less rustic trails on the other side of town.

I waited at the trailhead until Edith's purple boots were a tiny speck of color. Now that I knew her regular route, I didn't need to keep her in sight. In fact, it'd be better if I lost sight of her since she wouldn't spot me that way, either.

I lured Orion in close to my side and stuck to the center of the trail as much as possible. When Judith and I were twelve, we'd come out here to pick the wild black raspberries that grew along this particular trail. We'd come home covered in poison ivy.

Which begged the question—how far off the trail would Edith have been willing to go to harvest the hemlock? Every time I'd seen her walking, she'd been wearing boots.

This was probably a fool's errand. But if nothing else, Orion could use the extra exercise, so the walk wouldn't be a complete loss.

I examined the edges of the path as we walked. I did spot poison ivy, as well as poison oak, but no hemlock. We reached the fork in the trail where left would take us on the short path back to town and right would take us on the should-never-be-attempted-in-sandals trek.

My gut instinct about Edith was that she generally took the longer path simply because most other people didn't. It was nearly overgrown in some places. But that would also make it the ideal spot for her to pick hemlock. She wasn't as likely to be caught at it, and the longer path had the swampy part. According to the article I'd read, a specific type of hemlock enjoyed that environment.

The swampy portion wasn't far down the longer trail. I could go to that point and turn around. It couldn't add more than a quarter of a mile to the walk. A half mile at most.

Orion had his head into a bush, sniffing and snorting.

I gave a gentle pull on his leash. "Heel."

He came to my side—reluctantly. Still a win. When I first got him, he would have already pulled me into that bush to investigate.

We started down the longer path. Branches scratched at my arms occasionally, and the air smelled like damp moss and decomposing leaves. All noises from town were blocked out by the dense trees. The only sounds instead were the leaves rustling together and far-off bird calls.

Orion walked along with his nose down, reminding me a bit of a Basset Hound following a lead. Probably of a fox or a raccoon.

Sumac and other plants I didn't recognize lined most of the path. I kept my gaze directed downward. The website said hemlock could grow quite tall, but the big ones probably weren't easy to pull out and hide in food. She'd have needed one the size of a parsnip.

We'd almost reached the part of the path where the trail was more sludge than solid. I couldn't cross it in flip flops. Not without risking a broken shoe and a bare-footed walk home.

Broken branches to the right caught my attention. It looked like someone had pushed their way through, off the path. My heart beat so hard in my chest that I felt shaky.

"Sit, Orion. Stay"

He plopped his bottom to the ground, his tail swishing. We'd been practicing this at home, but I hadn't field tested it in the real world yet. Here's hoping it worked. I didn't want him following after me and getting a tick. Bad enough that I might get a tick on me or poison ivy again.

I checked the forged path. Nothing that looked like poison ivy, poison oak, or poison sumac. Judith and I had memorized what they all looked like after our first encounter.

I eased my way in. It didn't go back far. Less than five feet.

The ground behind the bushes had been dug up. A few hemlock plants still edged the cluster.

Holy crap. I'd been right.

A scrap of orange and yellow fluttered in the breeze, stark against the green around it. I brushed it with my fingers. A scrap of fabric. It felt silky like the scarves Edith always wore.

I couldn't remember whether I'd seen her wearing this particular color and pattern before, but all I'd need to do was show a picture to Detective MacIntosh. He could hopefully get a warrant to search her house for the scarf. If she'd burned it or thrown it out—which is what I would have done if I'd realized the scarf I was wearing while collecting poison to murder someone had ripped while doing the deed—then he might be able to get the warrant to include the photos in her house, on her phone, and posted to her social media accounts. All they'd need was one picture of her wearing this scarf.

I pulled out my phone.

Behind me, Orion made a noise low in his throat, half growl, half bark.

I spun around. Edith stood on the edge of the path, blocking my exit, her heavy walking stick raised, ready to swing.

25

"You don't want to do this." Clearly a lie, since Edith had intended to bludgeon me from behind. My voice was half-shriek, half-gasp. "People know I'm here." Also a lie, but hopefully not obviously. "And everyone knows you walk this path regularly. If my body's found here, someone will put it all together."

Even that part was a stretch. I'd hadn't even told anyone that I suspected Edith. I didn't want to be the girl who cried wolf.

Edith shook her head like my attempt was almost amusing. "No one would assume I'd hurt you, especially if I call it in and tell the police I'd found you this way. I have no motive. In fact, everyone knows how grateful I am to you for saving Buddy. I'm the last one who'd want to hurt you."

No doubt she'd take her walking stick home and burn it first to destroy the blood evidence.

"Then why do it?" Maybe if I played dumb. She didn't absolutely know what I was doing here.

But my voice was shaking. Hard.

Edith's glance bounced from my phone to the scrap of fabric. She swung.

I screamed, dropped, and rolled. Brambles sliced my skin, and little trails of fire followed along behind them.

I threw my hands up to protect my face. Stupid move. Why hadn't I launched myself at Edith the way I had at Kat? Then at least I might have had a fighting chance.

Orion's quiet growl turned to a snarl. Edith screamed and didn't stop, and then Buddy was barking, high and sharp.

I opened my eyes and lowered my arms. Edith lay on the ground, Orion's jaws clamped around one of her arms.

A spasm went through my chest, and I couldn't get a full breath. No no *no*. She'd been swinging a large stick, one of Orion's triggers, and she'd been threatening me.

I hadn't taught him a command for this situation. We shouldn't have ever been in a situation where he felt threatened enough to defend himself or me. His whole body was shaking, the fur along the nape of his neck poker-stiff.

"Orion, release!" The command for him to give me the toy in his mouth.

He didn't move. The noises coming from him sounded more wolf-like than dog-like.

No blood seeped from where he held her. That had to be good. Maybe he hadn't torn the skin. Maybe he was only using his body as a barricade and making sure she didn't continue to pose a threat.

If I pulled at his collar, though, he might clamp down harder. Edith's scream had turned into a wail. What else could I try?

I leaped to my feet, picked up her walking stick, and heaved it as far as I could into the trees so that it wasn't still in his line of sight. My left flip-flop had broken. I kicked it off and backed up ten feet down the trail. Hopefully that would take me out of the equation, too.

"Orion, come!" His body language changed slightly, a slackening. "Come! Orion! Come!"

He let go of her and ran to me. He used his body as a blocker between us. His whole form quivered. I grabbed his leash.

Edith had sat up. She held her arm close to her chest, like a bird with a broken wing. Her cell phone was in her hand.

"I've been attacked," she yelled into it, "by a vicious dog on the Rockport Trail."

***

I rested my forehead on my arms, which now not only burned from the scratches but had broken out into a rash thanks to something I'd rolled through. The police interrogation table beneath my arms smelled vaguely of eraser and reminded me of when I'd been in elementary school and we'd had to stay in during recess, with our heads down, as punishment.

This had all gone so very wrong.

Bob Bremnes had come along with the officers who responded to Edith's 911 call. He'd muzzled Orion and taken him from me, apologizing in a whisper the whole time and promising me he'd call Judith.

Then the officers had put Edith and me into separate squad cars and driven us both down to the station to "take our statements." I'd asked for Detective MacIntosh. I insisted that I wouldn't talk to anyone else. He was the lead on Sebastian's death. It had to be him.

That'd been an hour ago. No one had come in to hear my side of the story, Detective MacIntosh or otherwise. Orion was probably so confused and frightened. It wasn't like Judith could come get him. If I had my phone, I could have at least called Maeve, but my phone was somewhere on Rockport Trail. Actually, by now my phone was probably in police custody, along with my broken flip flop.

The door to the room squeaked open.

I sniffed back the tears that were trying to escape and lifted my head.

Detective MacIntosh stood in the doorway, his suit impeccable as usual but his hair soft-looking without the usual gel. Had I forced them to call him in on his day off? That would *not* put him in a receptive mood.

His looked at me, and his eyes narrowed slightly.

"You look like you got into a fight with a tree, and the tree won."

I lifted a hand to my hair. It was thick, wavy, and borderline unruly on the best of days. Sure enough, my fingers hit something hard. I pulled a twig, complete with leaves, out of the top of my ponytail. "That's because she tried to kill me. Edith, I mean. Not a tree. Trees don't have genders."

I blurted out the whole story. Somewhere in the middle, he took a seat across from me. I included every detail I could think of.

He ran his fingers through his hair. It ruffled up and made him look a bit like a mad scientist. "Mayor Cameron is telling a vastly different story. According to her, she was out walking her dog when your dog broke loose and viciously attacked her without any provocation. She said that anything you might say otherwise was all an attempt to keep your dog from being euthanized."

I sucked in a breath. "She wants to kill Orion?" The words sounded strangely tinny and distorted in my ears, like I was trapped underwater. "It was self-defense. Or owner defense. He was defending me. It wasn't his fault."

He let out a long sigh. "It's your word against—"

This couldn't be happening. Not now. "Against hers. And she's the mayor, and I'm the woman with the sketchy childhood. And blood will tell."

A line appeared between Detective MacIntosh's eyes. "No. It's your words against the bruises on her arm."

My insides burned like a giant ball of flames. She'd killed Sebastian. She'd tried to kill Judith. Now she wanted to kill Orion, too. Did she think I was going to sit by while it happened? Or that I'd ever stop looking for proof? Or did she plan to create some unfortunate accident for me in the future?

I slapped a palm down on the table. "Send someone back to the woods."

"Dr. Stephens—"

"That scrap of fabric beside the spot where she dug up the hemlock proves that I'm telling the truth."

"Dr. Stephe—"

No, he had to listen to me. He had to. "Orion was abused before I got him. She was trying to kill me the same way he was beaten as a puppy. Was he supposed to let it happen?"

"Zoe." His voice was firm and calm despite the fact that I was practically yelling at him.

It was the first time he'd ever used my first name.

I tried to breathe deeply, but all I could get in were short gasps. My vision swirled as if my head were about to topple off my body.

Detective MacIntosh leaned forward. "You don't have to convince me. I believe you."

My chest opened up, and air rushed in like water through a broken dam. "You believe me?"

He nodded. "Just this once. Don't get used to it." A

flicker of a smile crossed his lips. "I've seen that dog of yours. He's no more dangerous than my dog. But the fabric isn't enough to prove anything. She walks that trail all the time. She can easily argue that she caught her scarf on a branch when she was on one of her walks after Sebastian died. Or even that it blew off her neck, and she lost it."

He was right. There were a hundred ways she could wiggle out of it. I hadn't intended that scrap of fabric to be definitive proof of her guilt. I thought it would be a starting place. It put her at a spot where she could have gotten the hemlock to poison Sebastian.

The police were supposed to have time after that to dig deeper. Orion's life wasn't supposed to be on the line.

Detective MacIntosh pressed his hands into the table. "Do you have anything else? Any way to prove she took the hemlock home with her?"

I wouldn't have had to follow her out into the woods if I'd had any way to link her more concretely to Sebastian's murder.

My throat closed, and tears pressed against the back of my eyes. All I wanted was to throw my arms around Orion's neck and breathe in his warm doggy scent and pretend like none of this had happened. *She* tried to kill *me*, not the other way around. It wasn't fair that Orion was locked away on death row, but Edith could go home with Buddy.

Wait! That was it! Buddy!

I met Detective MacIntosh's gaze. "Edith called the

Pet Poison Help Line when she couldn't reach me, when she thought Buddy had eaten something he shouldn't. I was annoyed with the person she spoke to because they had her give Buddy hydrogen peroxide. Giving a dog hydrogen peroxide without trained supervision is risky. They never would have told her to do that on a vague suspicion of *I think he ate something poisonous*. But they would if she'd told them Buddy ate hemlock. With his small size, his only hope would have been getting as much of it out of him as possible. If they record their calls, would that be enough evidence?"

Detective MacIntosh gave me a smile that was almost roguish. "That'd be exactly what we need."

26

Judith looked at me expectantly across the table, as if she'd asked me a question I'd missed. She probably had. It'd been two days since Edith attacked me in the woods, and there'd been no word from Detective MacIntosh since. How long could it possibly take to get a warrant for any information collected by the Pet Poison Help Line? At least an officer had returned my phone.

I'd gone on my lunch break today to eat with Orion. He practically knocked me over when he saw me, but the crying when I'd had to leave him was heart-wrenching—both mine and his.

Judith set her pen down on top of the pad of paper she'd been writing on. "Maybe we should do this later when..."

When this was all over? Who knew when that would be. If Detective MacIntosh couldn't prove Edith poisoned Sebastian, then I'd end up fighting to save Orion from being euthanized. This could drag on for months, not to mention the stress of knowing Sebastian's murderer was walking around free.

I shook my head. "This is important, too. Besides, I need something to distract me. Just remind me where we were."

"We have the police officers from Toledo who are willing to bring their dogs and do a presentation. Now we have to convince the school board."

"Right."

My brain clicked back into the task. After what had happened at the council meeting with the breed ban, I'd decided Keith was right. It wasn't my place to force people who were scared to do what I wanted. A lot of people like Edith had bad experiences. Dogs did sometimes bite people.

If I ever wanted Arbor's law to change, breed-specific laws everywhere to change, it needed to start with giving people more information. Judith and I had decided the best way to do that was to show people, especially the children who would grow up to be the next generation of lawmakers, that the so-called dangerous breeds weren't necessarily dangerous by nature. We wanted to help teach them that even dogs with a bad past could often be rehabilitated.

The Toledo narcotics unit had two pit bulls they'd rehabbed after the dogs were rescued from a dogfighting ring. Two of their officers were willing to cross state lines and come all the way up here to help us. Judith said the officer she'd spoken to actually sounded excited to tell people how they'd retrained the dogs and how the dogs helped them now.

But we didn't know where we stood on support from the school board. "I think Maeve would be willing to help convince the school board. What's our next—"

The chords of "Joyful, Joyful We Adore Thee" rang through the house, signaling someone at the door.

Judith was already tapping something into her phone, probably searching for our next lead. Bob Bremnes from the shelter said he'd heard about another dog rescued from a dogfighting ring who was now working with firefighters to detect arson.

We might never get the law changed in Arbor, but if we didn't, that would have to be okay. I had to respect other people's differences in a case where it wasn't a moral issue. All I could do was show them the other side and let them make their own decisions.

As much as I'd rather it was different.

I opened the front door, and Orion lunged inside, his whole body wagging, happy squeaks coming from his throat. I ran my hands all over him as he tried to lick my arms and legs.

"Orion!" Judith squealed from somewhere behind me.

He swiped me once more with his tongue and then sprinted in Judith's direction.

I finally looked up. Detective MacIntosh stood on

the threshold.

"You're not Bob," I said.

I cringed internally. Just when I thought I couldn't embarrass myself more. What I'd meant was that I'd expected someone from the shelter to have brought Orion back, not Detective MacIntosh. But if I explained that now it might sound like I was criticizing him.

"Not according to my driver's license." He gave an almost-smile. "Disappointment is a bitter thing. I didn't want to get your hopes up until I was sure."

I glanced over my shoulder to where Judith was getting her face washed by Orion and laughing. "He's home for good?"

Detective MacIntosh nodded.

I threw my arms around him in a hug. He stiffened.

Heat blistered my cheeks. Oh, crap. What did I just do? This man wasn't a friend. He was a police officer. The endorphins from getting Orion back must have temporarily clouded my brain.

I dropped my arms and slowly stepped back. "Sorry. Got a little carried away there."

He straightened his tie. A touch of pink brightened his neck.

"We got the warrant for the Pet Poison Help Line records yesterday evening," he said as if nothing had happened, though his tone was a bit more formal than usual. "Mayor Cameron didn't give them her name, so she probably assumed she was safe to call. What she didn't realize is that they can see the phone number a person is calling from, and they do record that into their log. According to the employee's notes, she said that her dog ate stew from her garbage that she'd *accidentally* added hemlock to, mistaking it for wild parsnips."

The muscles in my jaw tensed. Of course she wouldn't have admitted to the truth even if she thought the call was anonymous. She was too smart for that. But it did prove that she had collected hemlock at some point. Could it have actually been an accident? But that wouldn't have explained Judith's car. Unless that really wasn't connected.

An ache built in my forehead. Too many questions rattled around in my brain. After all this, if she got away with what she'd done...

Orion pushed his head against my hand, and I stroked down his neck. Whatever else happened, I'd gotten him back, and Detective MacIntosh said it was permanent. Edith had given up her complaint against him. "Is that enough to arrest her for Sebastian's murder?"

Detective MacIntosh shook his head. A full smile took over his lips. My breath caught slightly in my throat. Good gracious, the man was handsome when he smiled.

"I told her that the Pet Poison Help Line records calls for safety and quality control purposes. I said it'd be easy enough to use voice recognition software to prove she was the one who placed the call, in addition to her phone number logged with the recording."

Almost every company you called these days had that warning about calls being recorded. "And she confessed once she heard it?"

His smile grew, crinkling his eyes at the corners. "There was no recording."

That was smart. I wouldn't have thought of it. "You lied."

His shoulders stiffened, and the smile vanished. "Lying is part of the job."

Touchy. But, then again, my words could have come across as accusatory. I held my hands up quickly then pressed them to my chest. "No judgment. I was impressed."

His shoulders relaxed, but his smile didn't return. The room felt strangely colder without it.

"She did confess and agree to drop her complaint against Orion in exchange for a plea deal. Apparently, she showed up at Sebastian Clunes' door with a bowl of stew 'as a peace offering' and said she wanted to discuss a compromise to the breed ban. She let him believe she'd be willing to back him in overturning the ban as long as those breeds had to be kept leashed or in yards at all times and their owners attended obedience classes with them."

It was almost exactly what I'd suggested to her as a compromise, and she shot it down. Sebastian or Judith had probably proposed the same thing to her long before.

"I'm recommending to the district attorney that they

make mandated therapy sessions part of her sentencing." His expression looked sad, almost as if he pitied Edith. "She was rambling about how she couldn't ever agree to that because the dog that bit her was supposed to be locked in a yard, but he got loose."

Tim Gilpin's pit bull escaping from his yard and the massive push to overturn the breed ban in response must have been the trigger that pushed her over the edge. It made her believe that her daughter could be hurt the way she had, and that she had to do everything in her power to keep her child safe.

I peeked at Judith again. Orion had returned to her, and she was scratching the spot on his neck that made him kick a back leg in the air. As much as I didn't agree with what Edith had done, I could understand the desire to protect the people you loved. "Did she confess to cutting Judith's brakes, too?"

He nodded. "Her husband showed her."

My stomach clenched, and an image of their daughter flashed across my mind. I'd only seen her the one time, on the sidewalk, holding Buddy's leash. Would she end up in foster care if both her parents went to prison, or would she have a relative who'd take her in the way I'd had? I'd been so blessed that my dad wanted me. I couldn't imagine what it would have been like to take all my anger and assumptions into foster care. "Will her husband get a lighter sentence?"

Maybe he could at least be out before his daughter turned eighteen.

Detective Macintosh frowned, and then his forehead smoothed. "Her husband wasn't part of it. She asked him to show her the brake lines because she claimed she was afraid. She told him she wanted to know how to check her own lines in case someone cut them, what with everything that was happening in town."

Judith rolled up beside me. "Would you like to come in and have a cup of coffee, Ryan, rather than standing on the doorstep?"

The corner of his mouth twitched just slightly. "Thank you for the offer, but there's paperwork waiting for me back at the station. I just wanted to..." He reached into the house and rubbed Orion's ear in the way that long-time dog lovers seemed to instinctively default to. "You know."

"Thank you for everything," Judith said.

I mentally kicked myself. I should have thanked him. If he hadn't believed me and listened to me in the end, things might have ended up differently. Hopefully my impulsive hug at least let him know I was grateful.

My phone rang on the table where I'd left it. I glanced at the clock on the wall. Six-thirty. On Tuesday. I'd forgotten all about my phone appointment with my grandfather's estate lawyer.

Detective Macintosh nodded at both of us. "I'll let you get that."

I closed the door and bounded to the phone. Orion must have thought it was a game because he launched after me and got the zoomies around the table.

I answered the FaceTime call. "Hello?"

A woman's face filled the screen. "This is Danica Dickerson with Page and Sketchley. Am I speaking to Zoe Stephenson?"

"That's me." My throat suddenly felt like it was made of sandpaper. I didn't have anything to be nervous about. Anything my grandfather left me would be more than I had before. But if it was enough, it would mean I could take Maeve up on her offer of becoming a partner in the clinic. "Judith's here, too."

"Is Judith your significant other?" Her voice had that slightly distracted tone that people got when they were preparing to write down an important piece of information.

Oh, she thought... "No, sorry, Judith's my sister. Judith Dawson."

Judith raised her eyebrows at me. Ms. Dickerson was quiet on her end of the line.

I leaned closer to the screen. Maybe she hadn't heard me. "You said my grandfather left everything to my sister and me."

"I did. Let me check one thing." She rifled through some papers. "The name I have for your sister isn't Judith, though. It's Harper."

A buzzing noise filled my ears. "What last name?"

"I..." Ms. Dickerson's voice faltered. "I'd assumed Stephenson like yours since your grandfather didn't say otherwise."

If Tonya had another child, her last name wouldn't

be Stephenson. I had my dad's last name because my parents were together when I was born, even though they weren't married.

When I was three, my dad became a Christian, and he'd wanted to get married. That's apparently when the fights started between them. Getting married was only the first change my dad wanted to make to their lifestyle. No more drugs was another.

Tonya had left him shortly after, and she took me with her. Because Tonya had never been arrested on a drug charge at that point, my dad wasn't able to get custody of me. Tonya barely let me see him after he tried. It wasn't until her arrest that everything changed.

Could Tonya have had another child after I was taken from her? If so, she hadn't told my dad about her. My half-sister would have ended up in foster care when my mom went to prison the second time. "Are you sure?"

More noises of papers moving around even though they weren't on screen this time. "Your mother's name is Tonya Crawford? Grandfather William Crawford?"

All I could get out was an affirmative "Umhumm."

"Then I'm certain. Your grandfather left his estate to you and a sister by the name of Harper."

The buzzing noise in my head became so loud that I couldn't focus on what Ms. Dickerson said next.

Somewhere out there, I had another sister. And I had to find her.

LETTER FROM THE AUTHOR

Thank you for coming along on this new adventure with me (and with Zoe). I've been dreaming about this series for a long time because I wanted to combine my love of writing with my love of animals. I'm a big advocate for adopting from shelters and for making sure that the dogs and cats in your life are spayed or neutered.

The next book in the Cat and Mouse Whodunits is available now! Zoe will be hunting for her newly discovered sister, while trying to solve a mystery involving Bob Bremnes, Judith's friend and fellow shelter employee.

If you haven't yet signed up for my newsletter, please do. I announce new releases there first, as well as sharing recipes and other fun bonuses. I also give my newsletter subscribers a free ebook copy of *Sapped*, a Maple Syrup Mysteries prequel.

You can sign up at www.smarturl.it/emilyjames.

Love,
Emily

ABOUT THE AUTHOR

Emily James grew up watching TV shows like *Matlock*, *Monk*, and *Murder She Wrote*. (It's pure coincidence that they all begin with an M.) It was no surprise to anyone when she turned into a mystery writer.

Alongside being a writer, she's also a baker, an animal lover, and a musician.

Emily and her husband share their home with a Boxer mix, nine cats (all rescues), and a budgie (who is both the littlest and the loudest).

If you'd like to know as soon as Emily's next mystery releases, please join her newsletter list at www.smarturl.it/emilyjames.

Made in United States
Troutdale, OR
02/29/2024

18089834R00184